Steampunk Wonderland

Photography by Stacy J. Garrett

Acknowledgements

This crazy adventure couldn't have happened without the help of my wonderful friends who, when told I wanted to do a steampunk Wonderland tea party, merely asked where they should meet me. Monarch Creations came through on the costumes, and the March Hare lent us her living room.

To Lily, Theresa, Bobby, Lindy, Dawn, Laura, and Sean: you guys are the best friends a photographer could have. Here's to future adventures together!

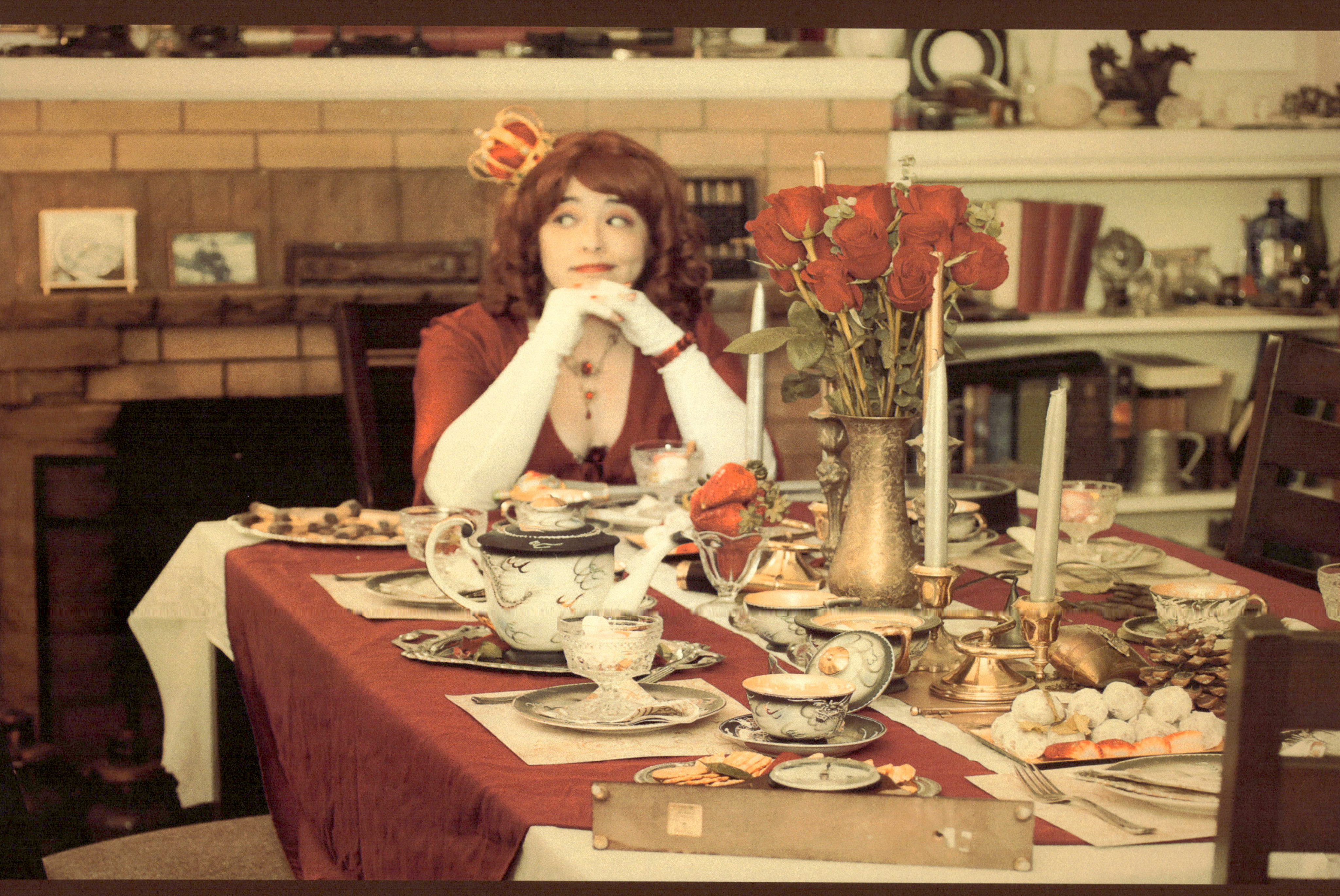

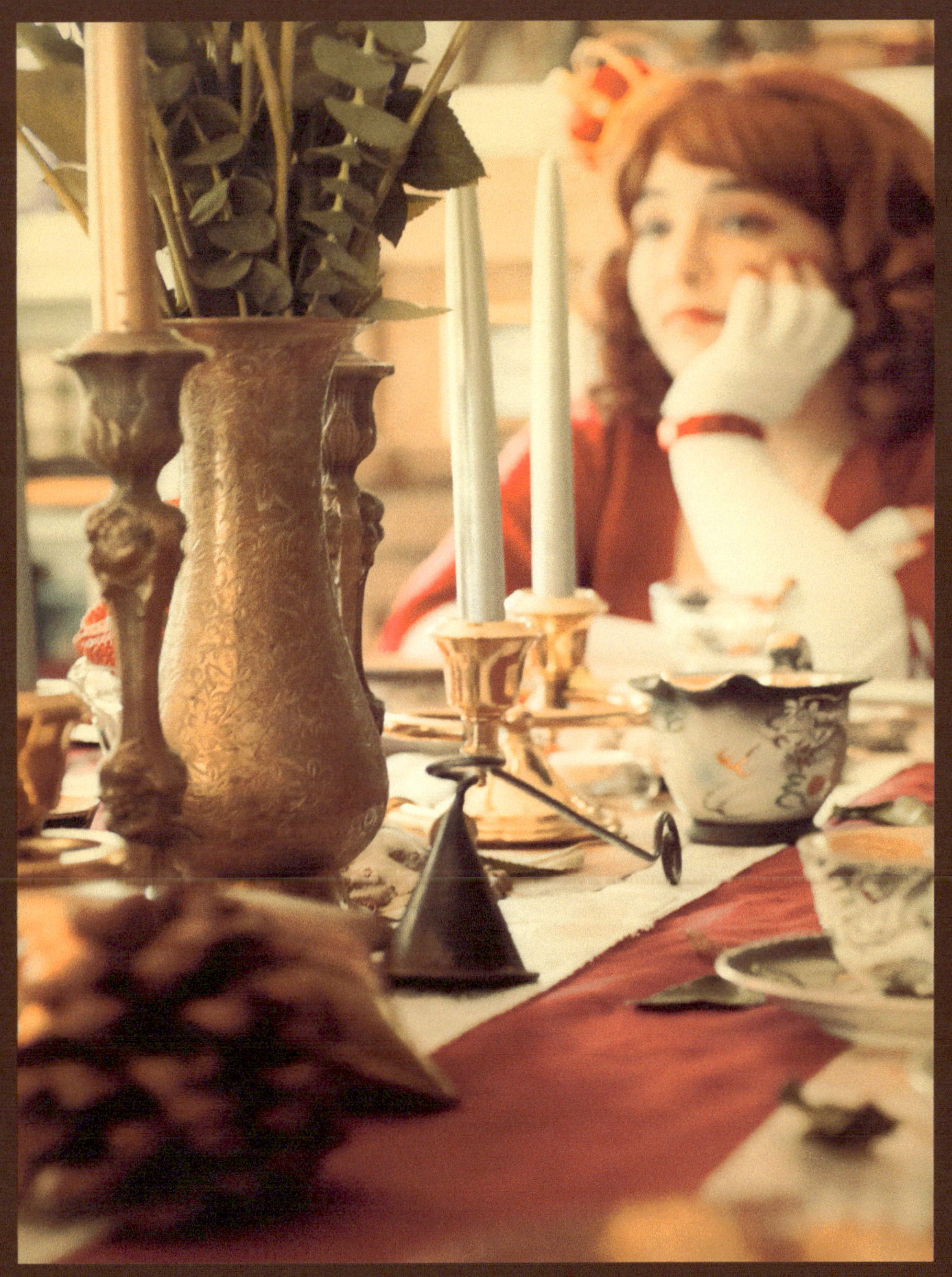

"Where is everyone?"

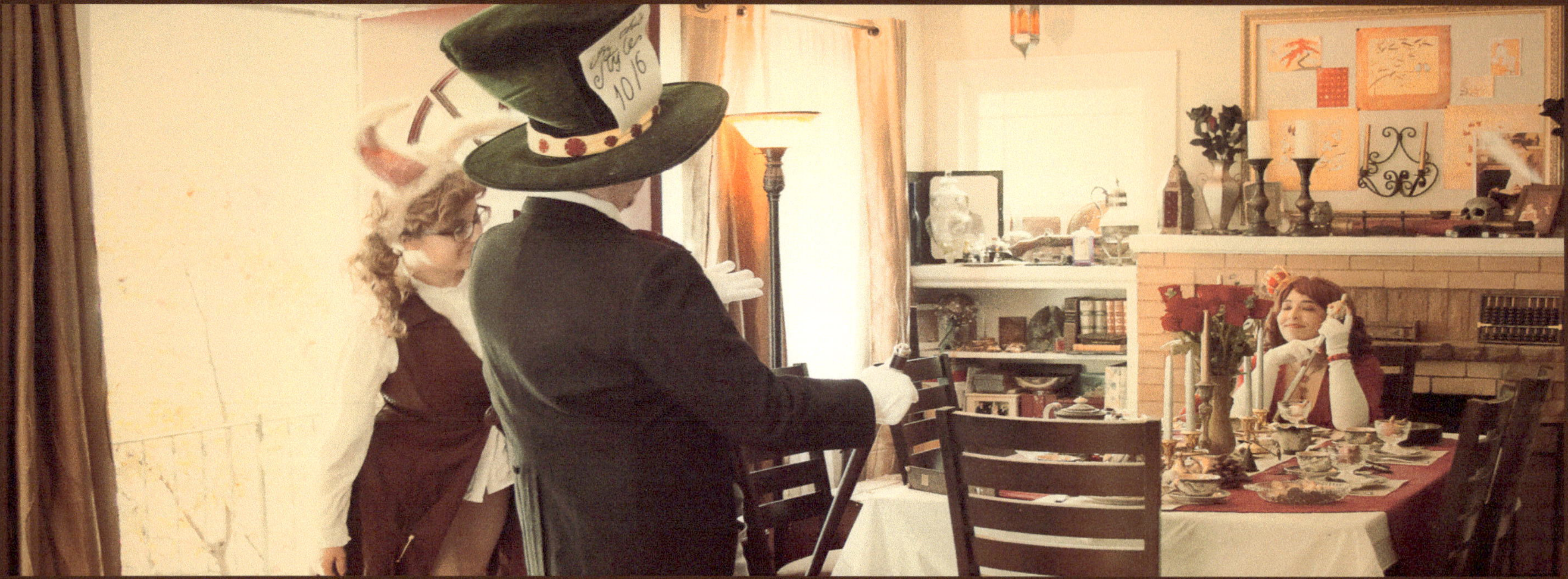

10/6

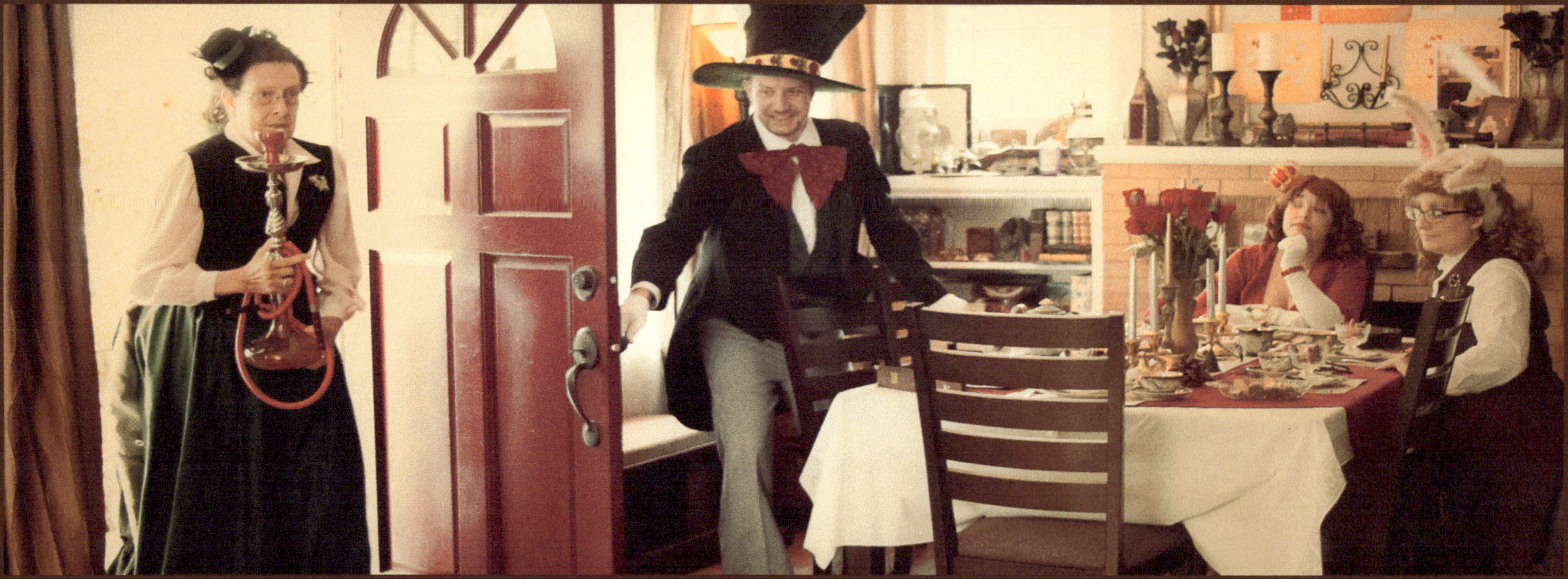

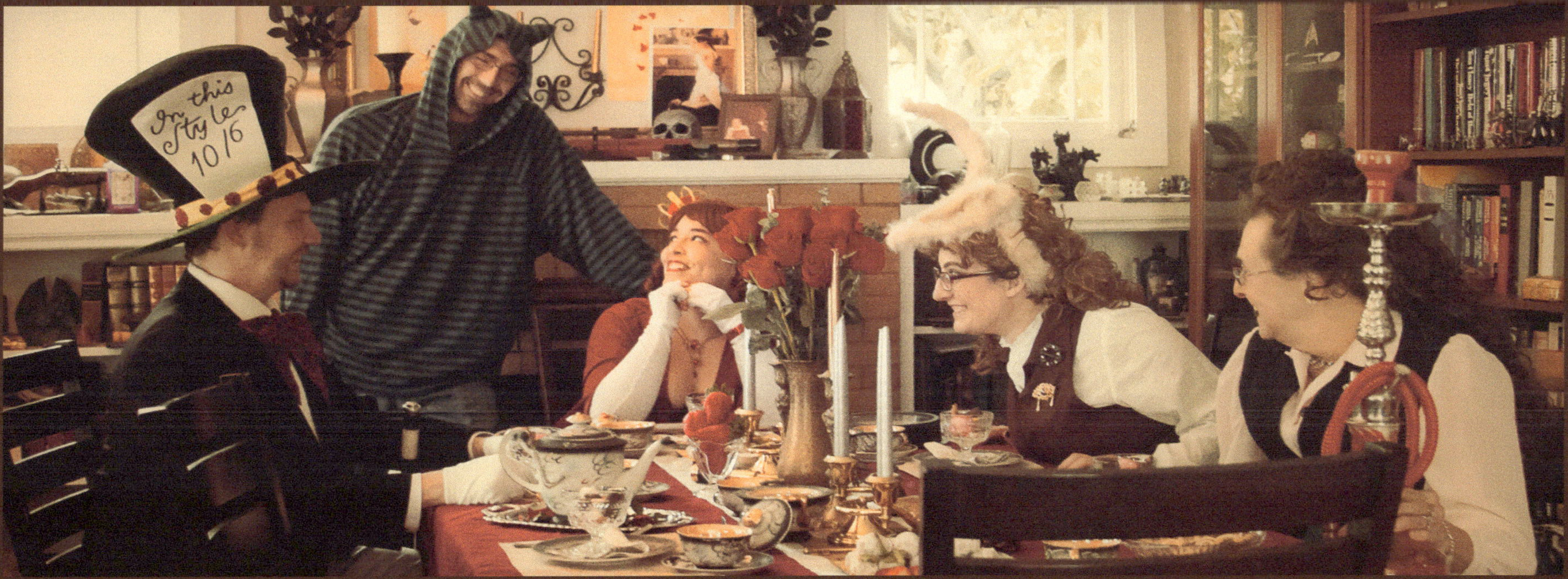

In this
Style
10/6

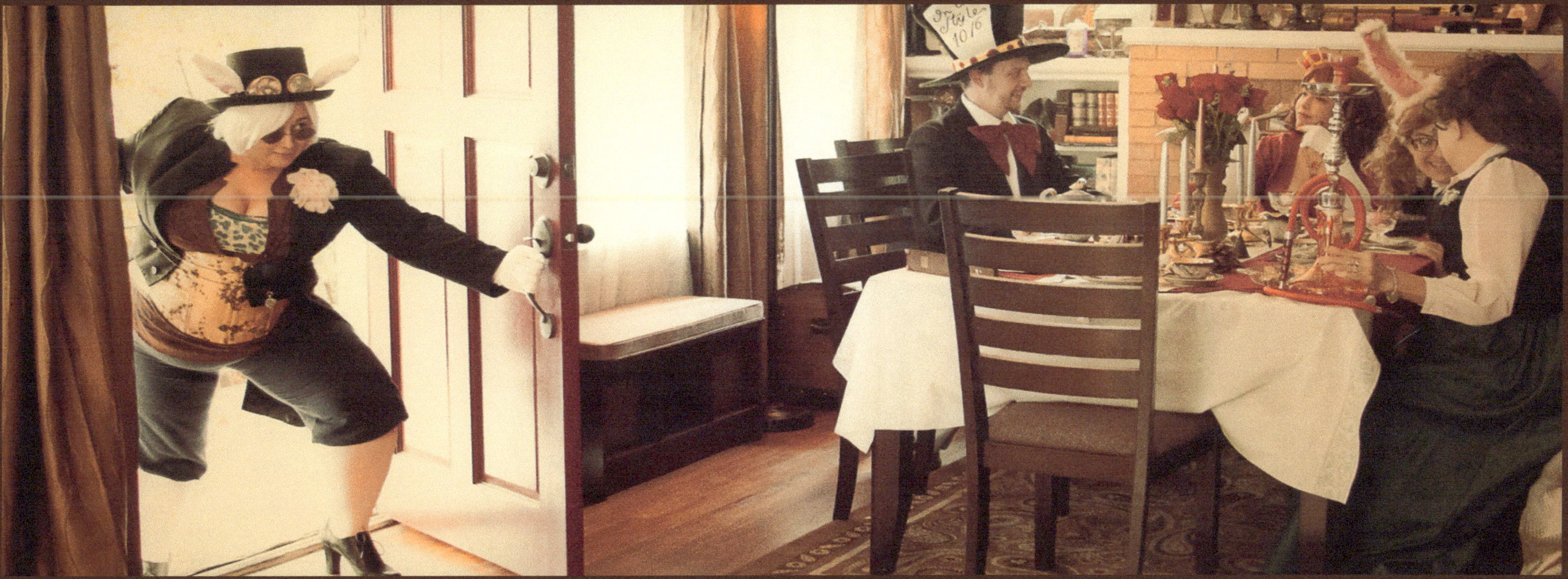

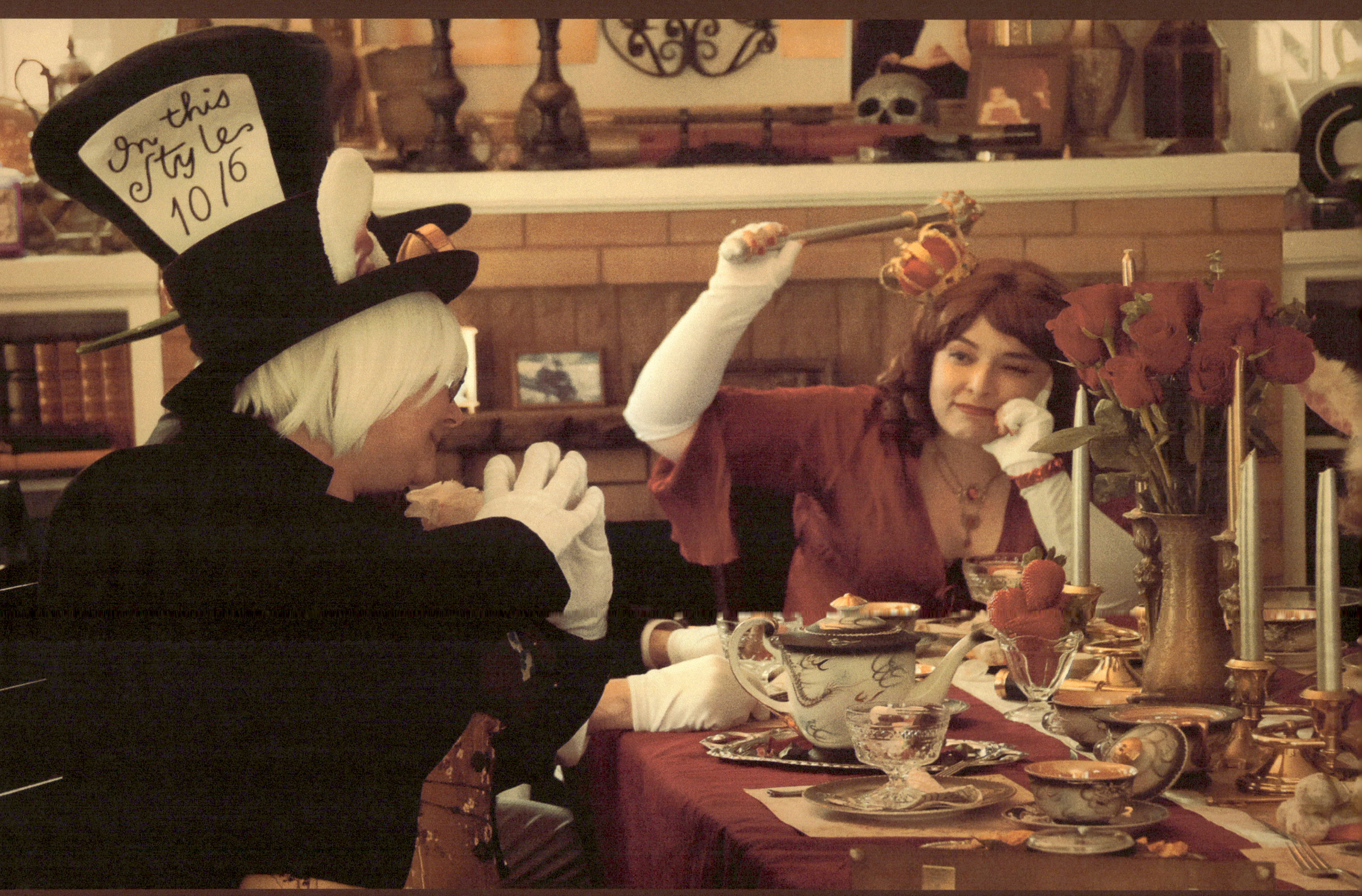
In this
style
10/6

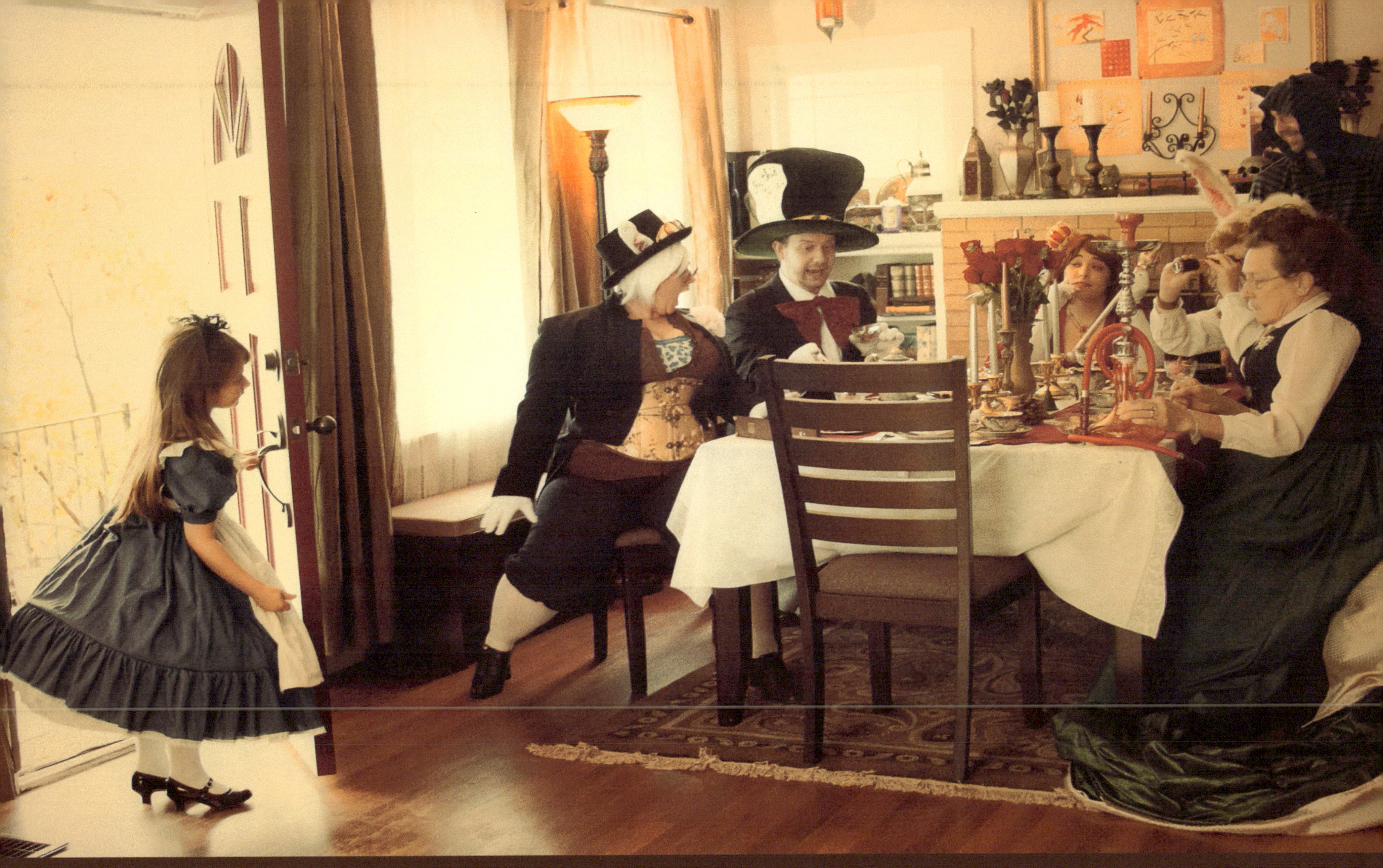

"Who are you?"
"Who am I? Where am I?"
"Well, if you don't know the first, we can't help you with the rest! Sit and have some tea."

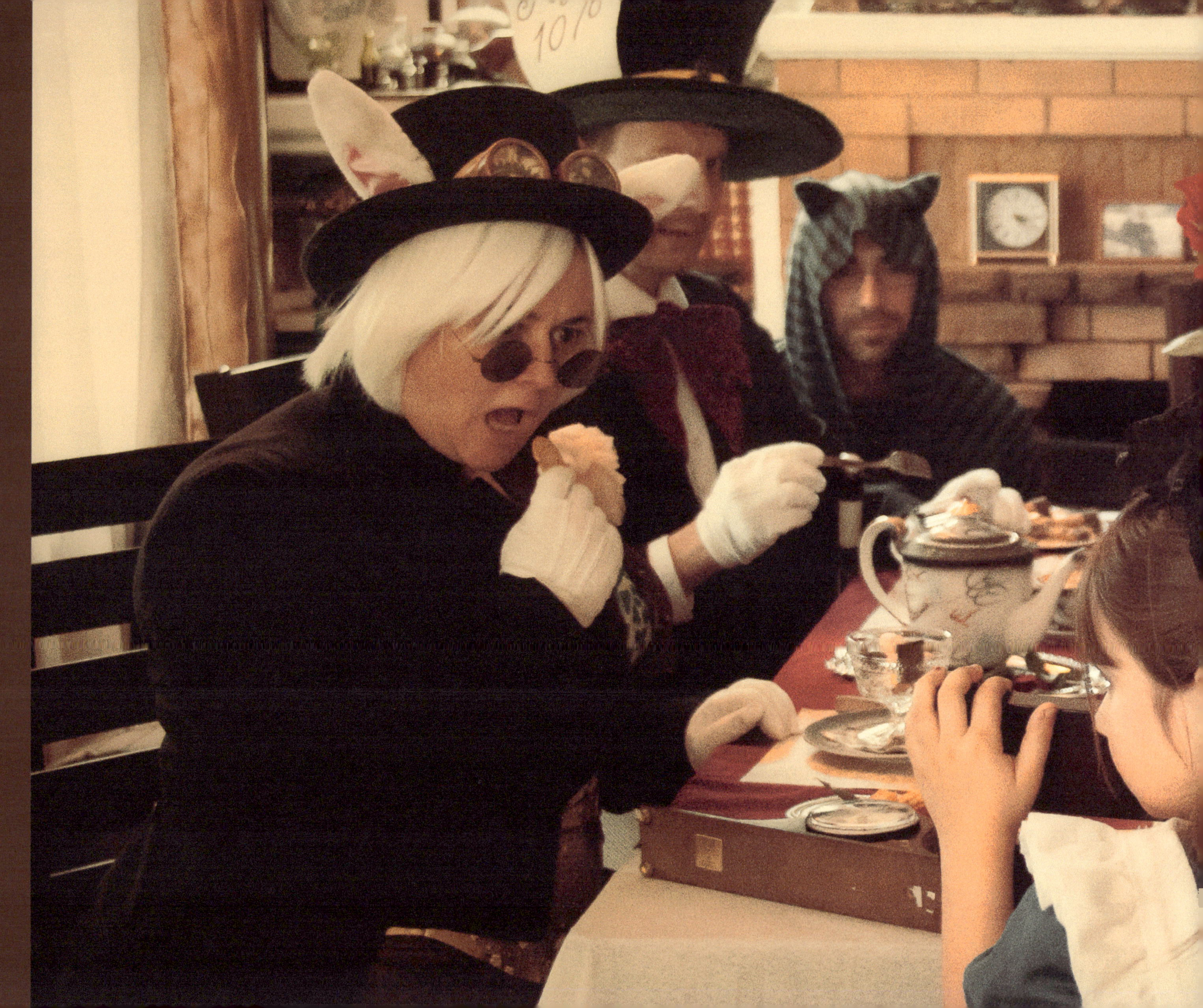

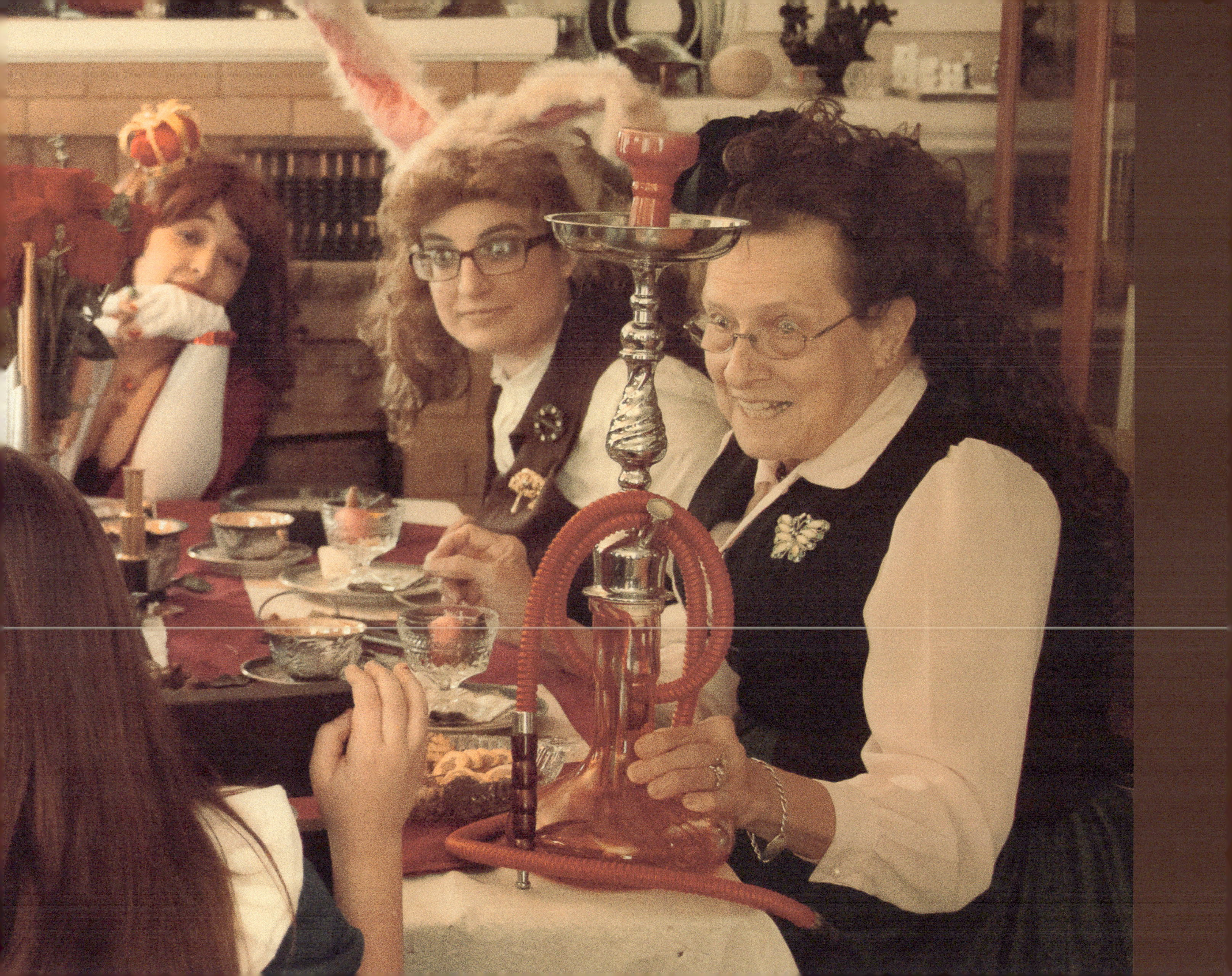

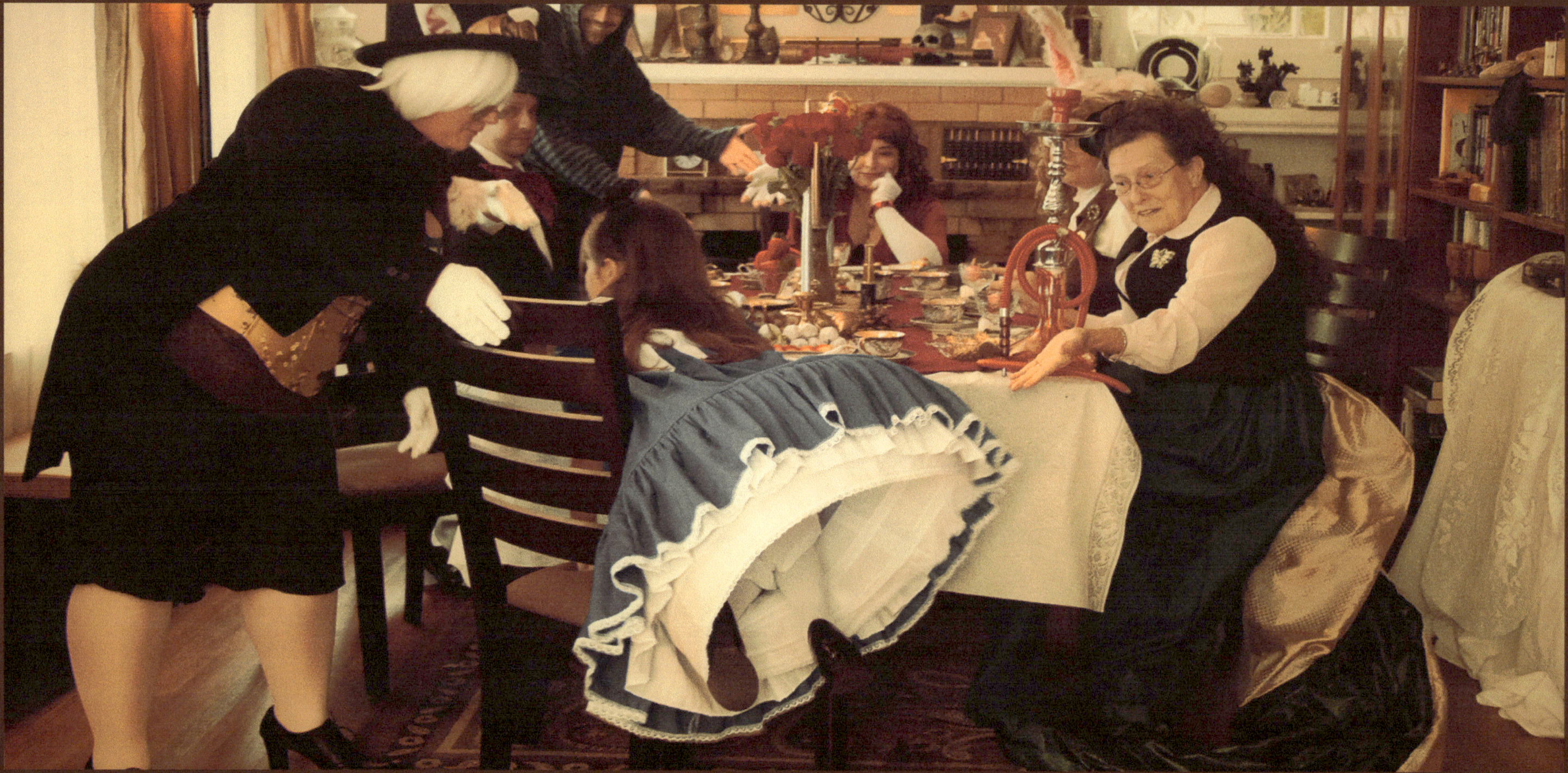

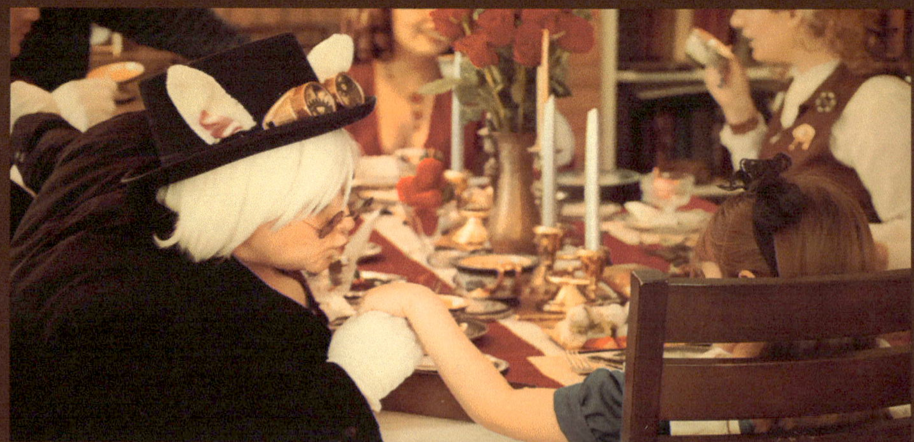

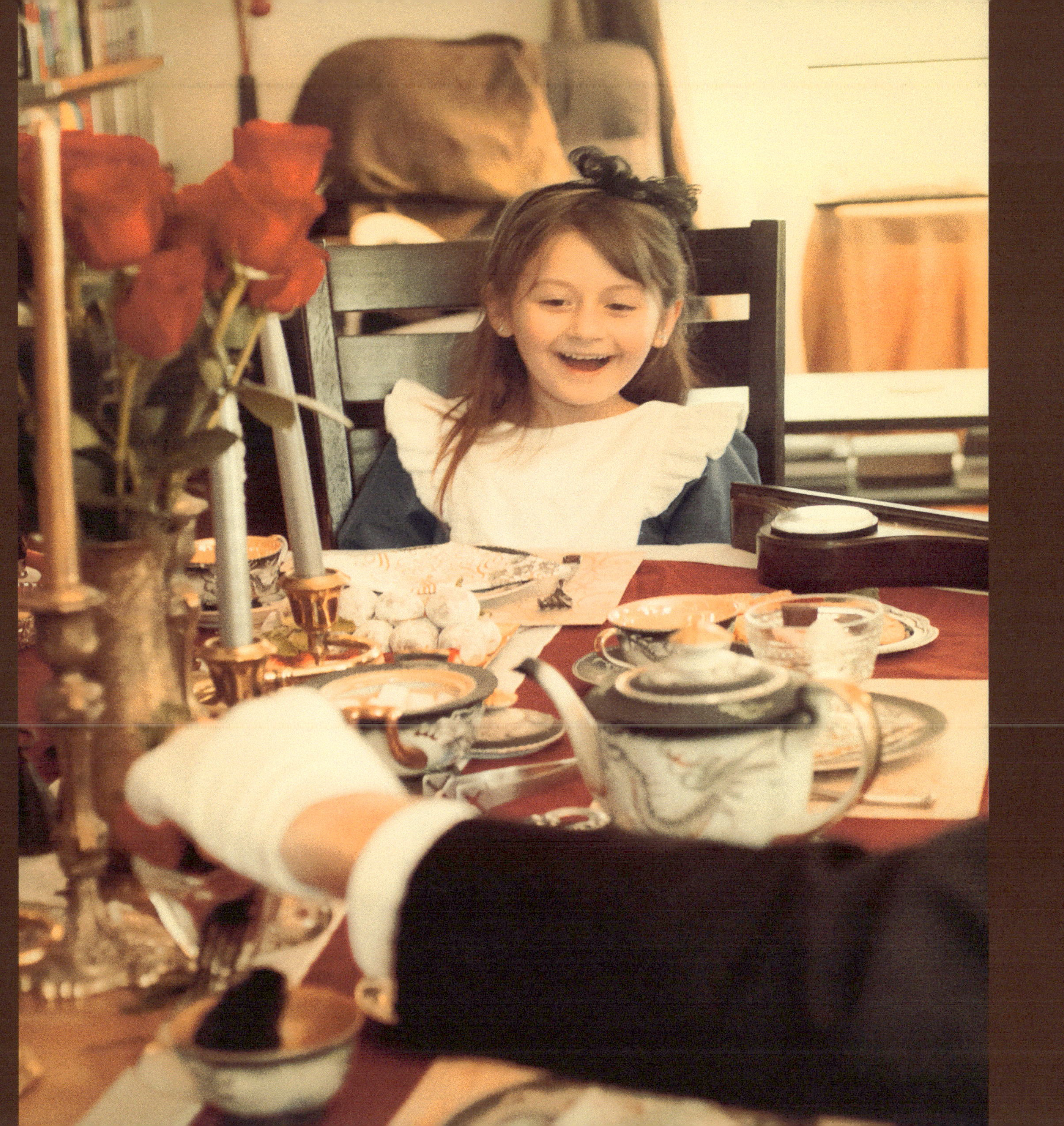

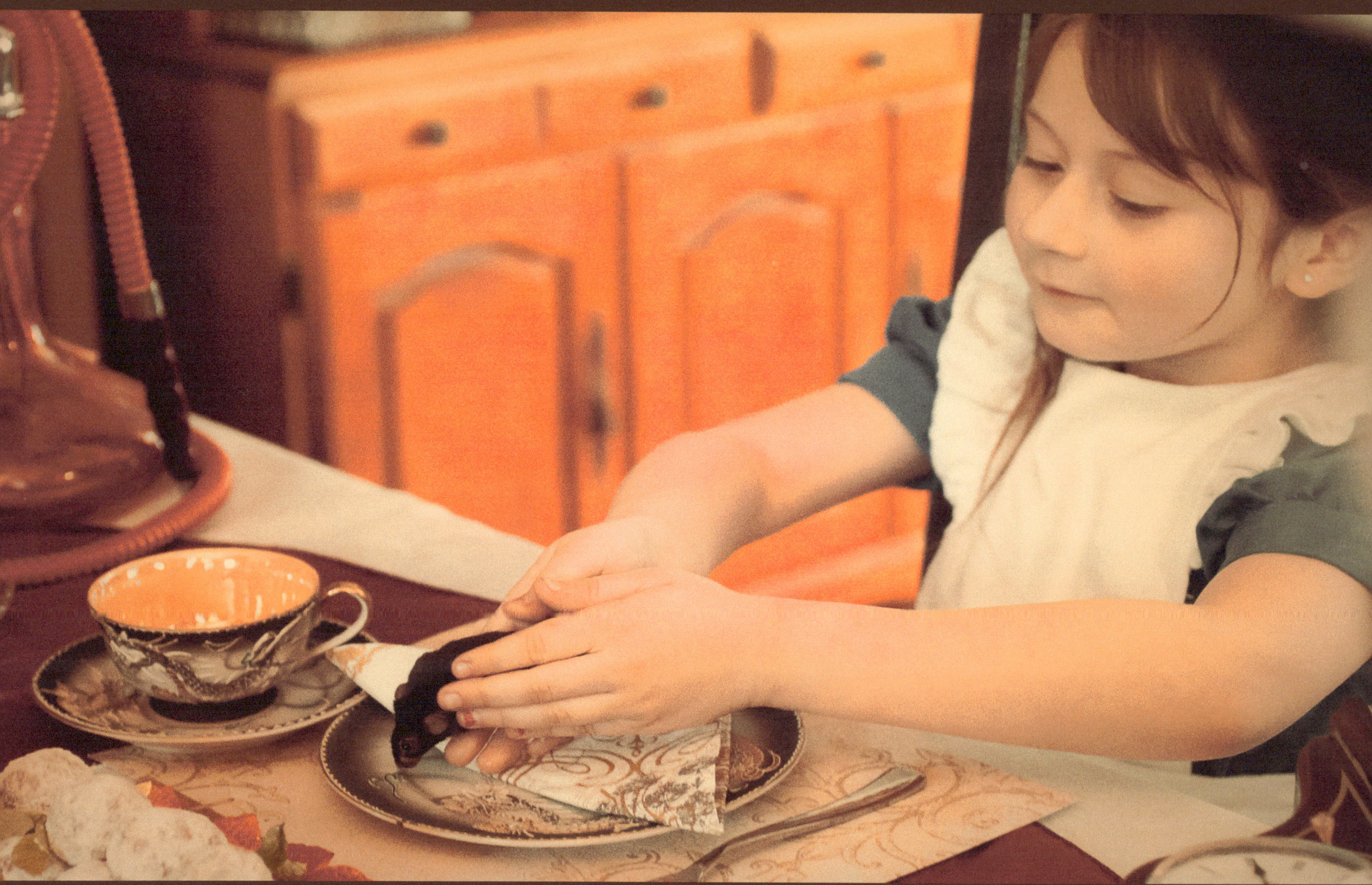

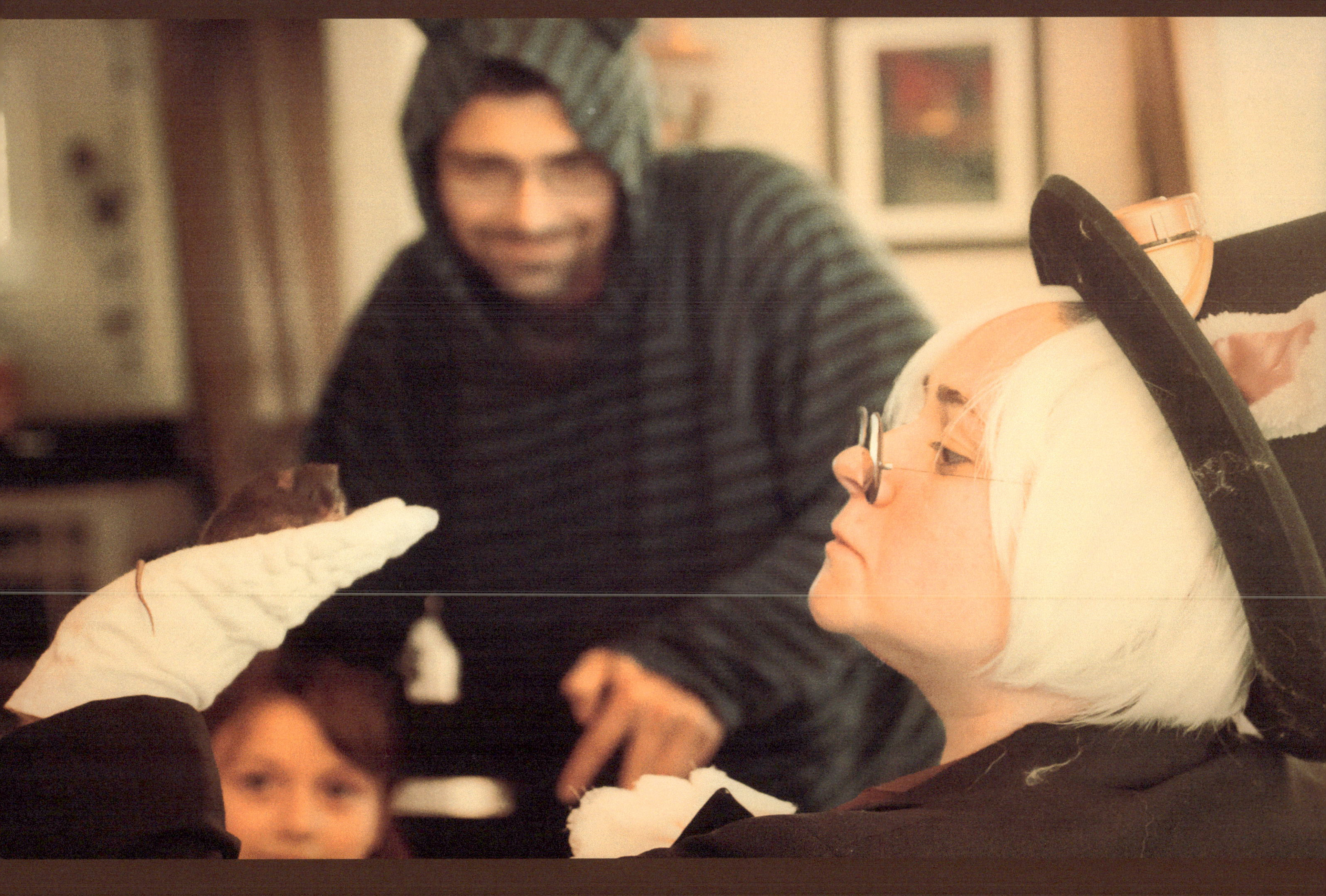

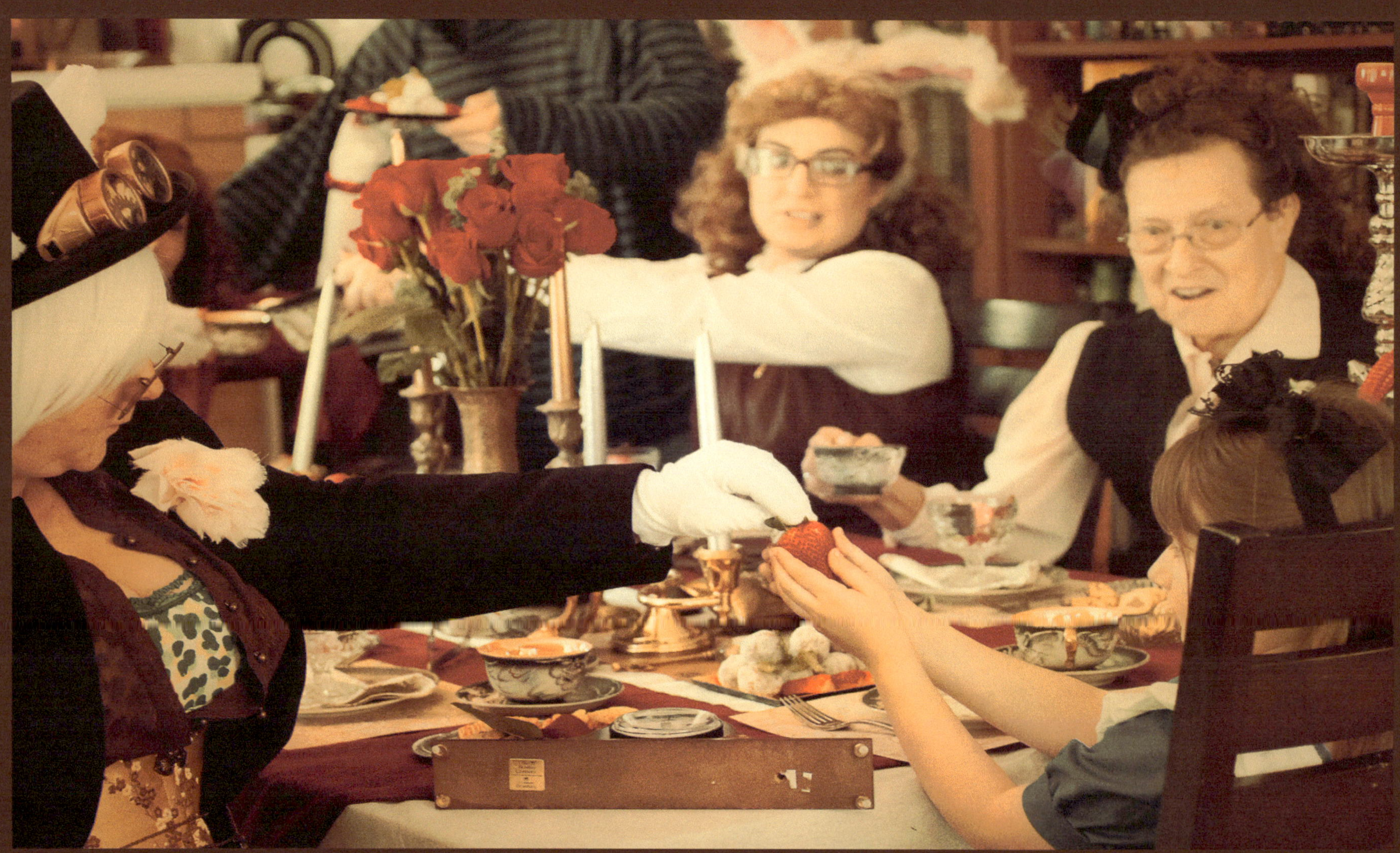

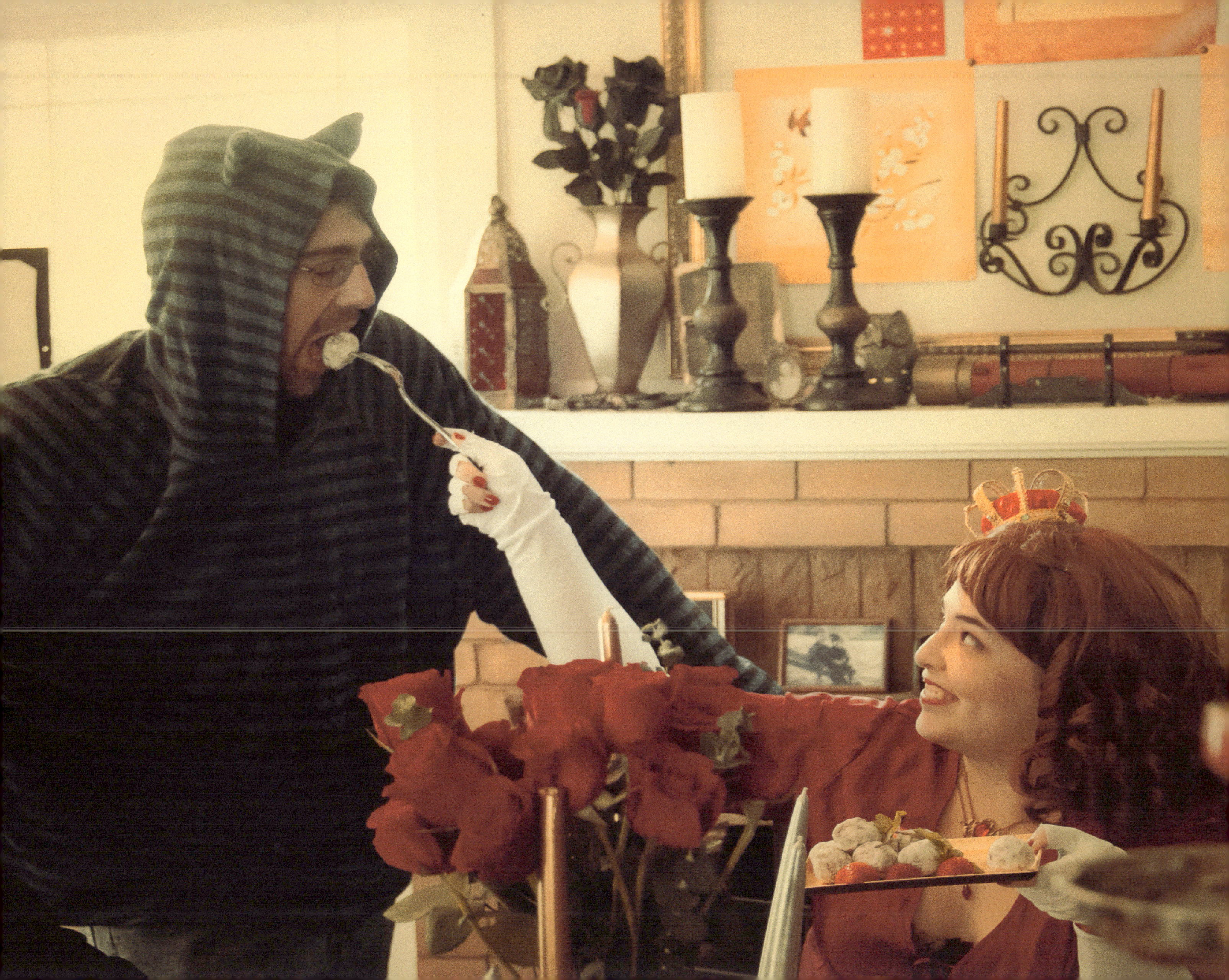

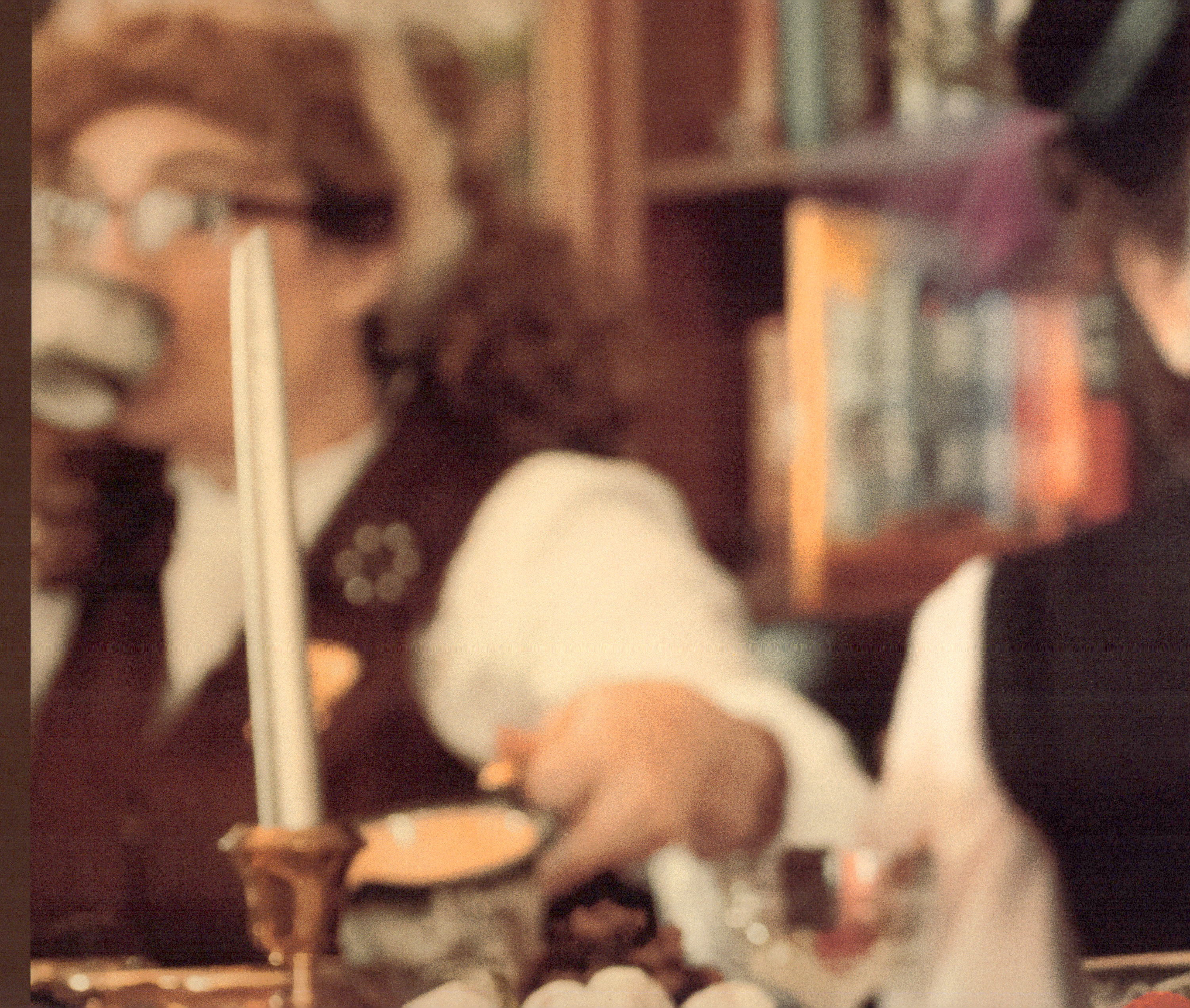

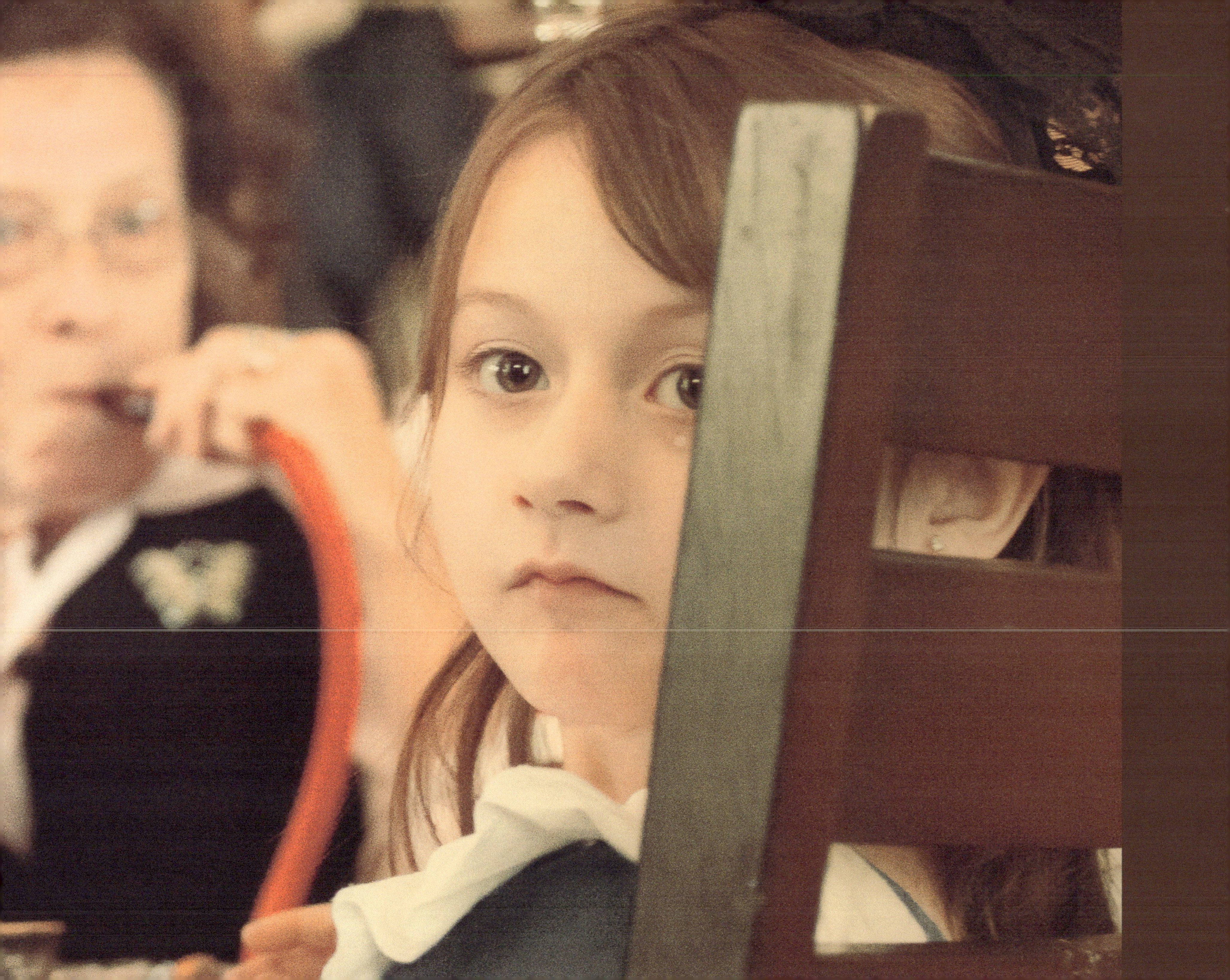

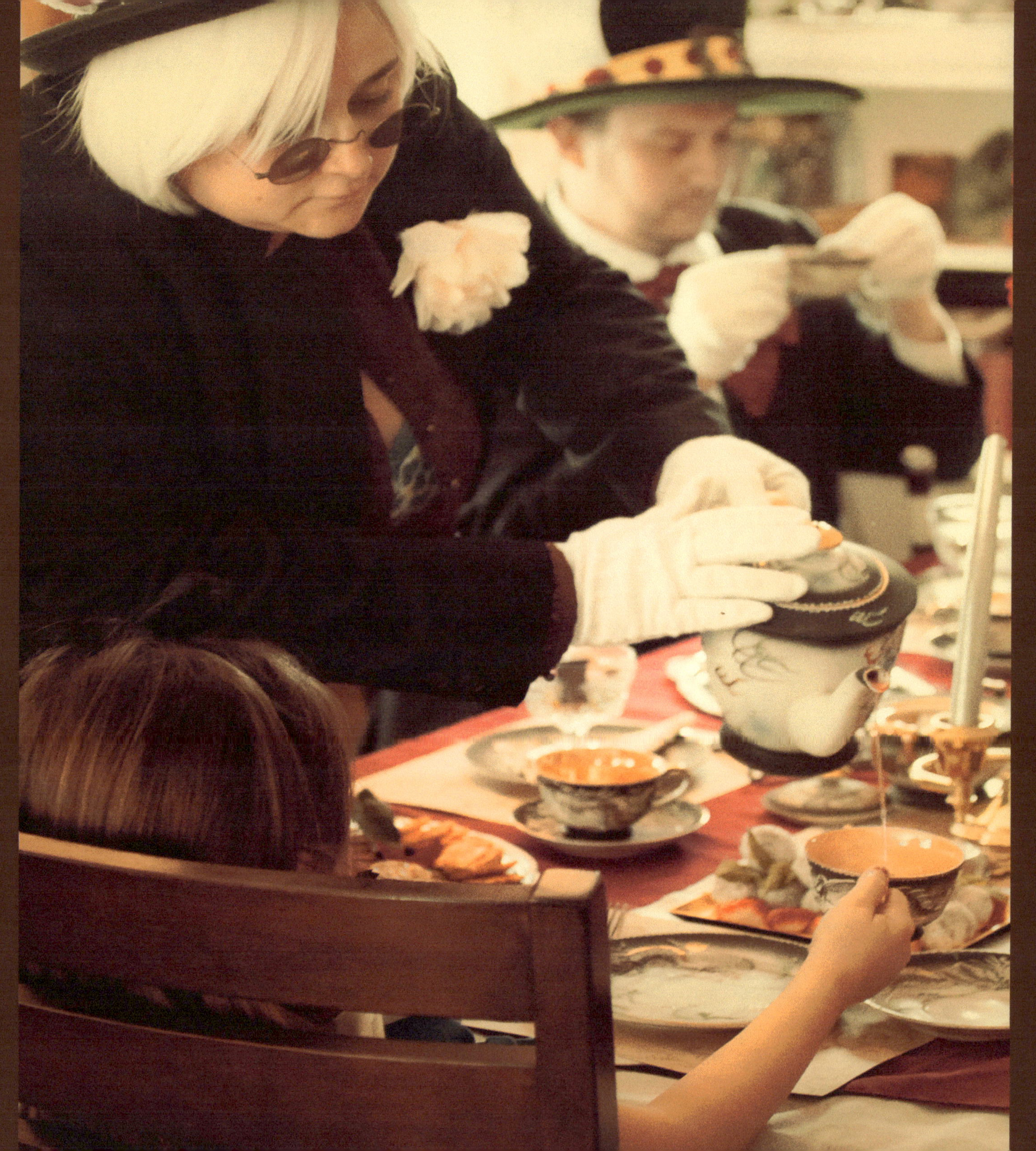

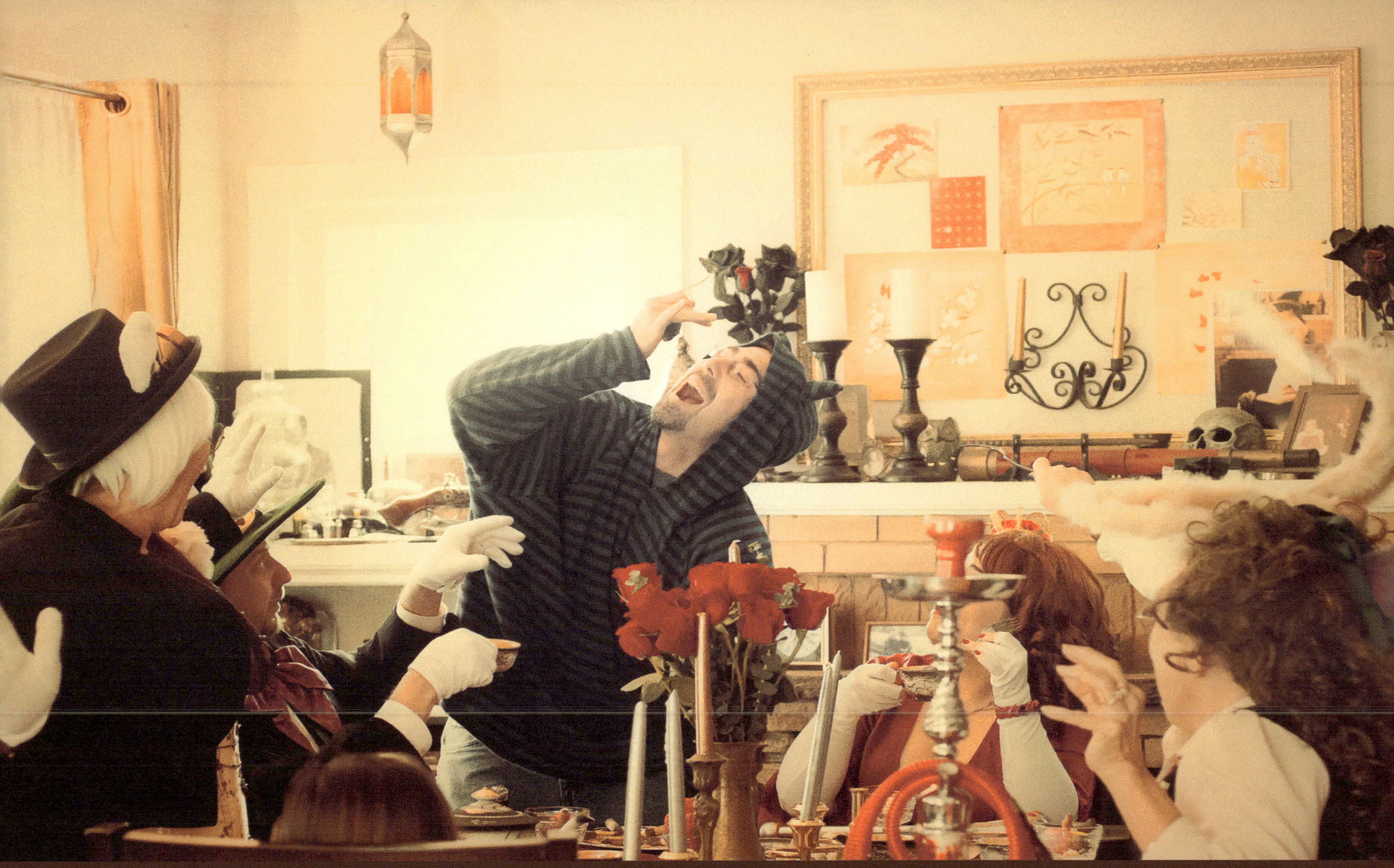

"Don't eat Dormouse!"
"Bad cat! Who invited him anyway?"

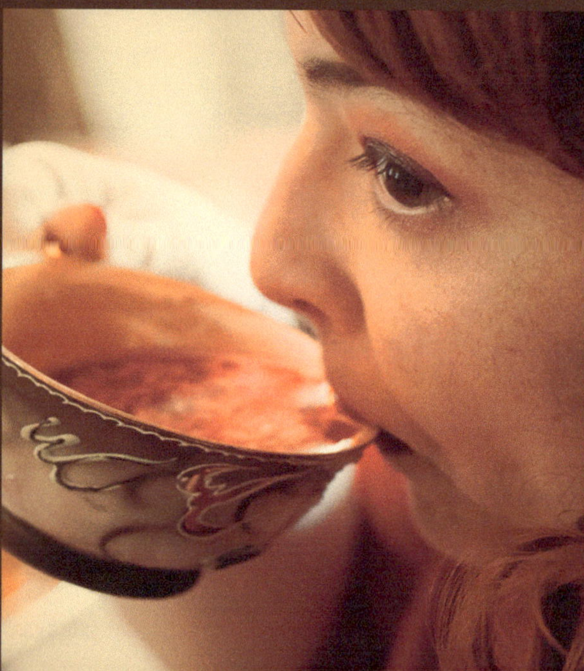

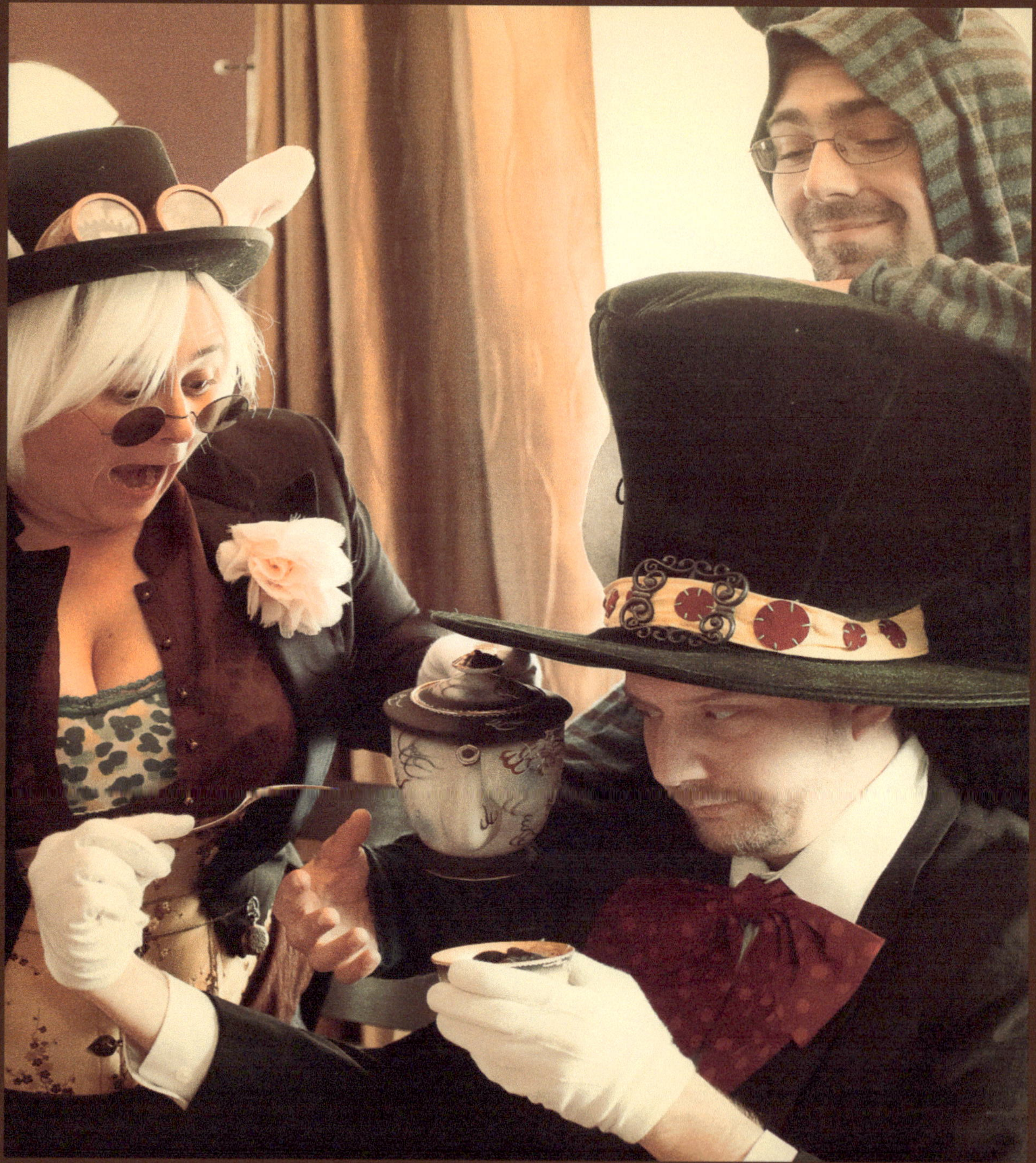

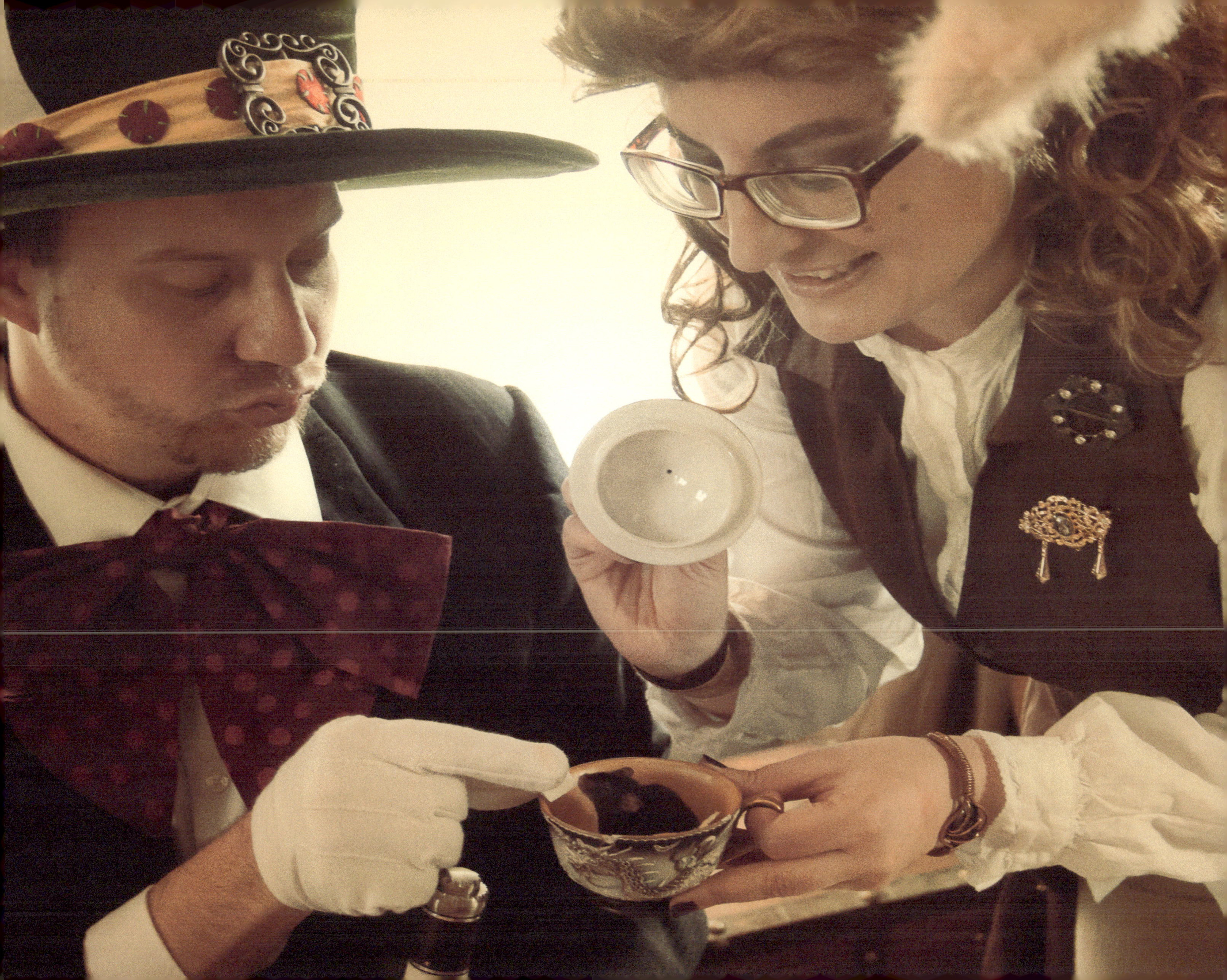

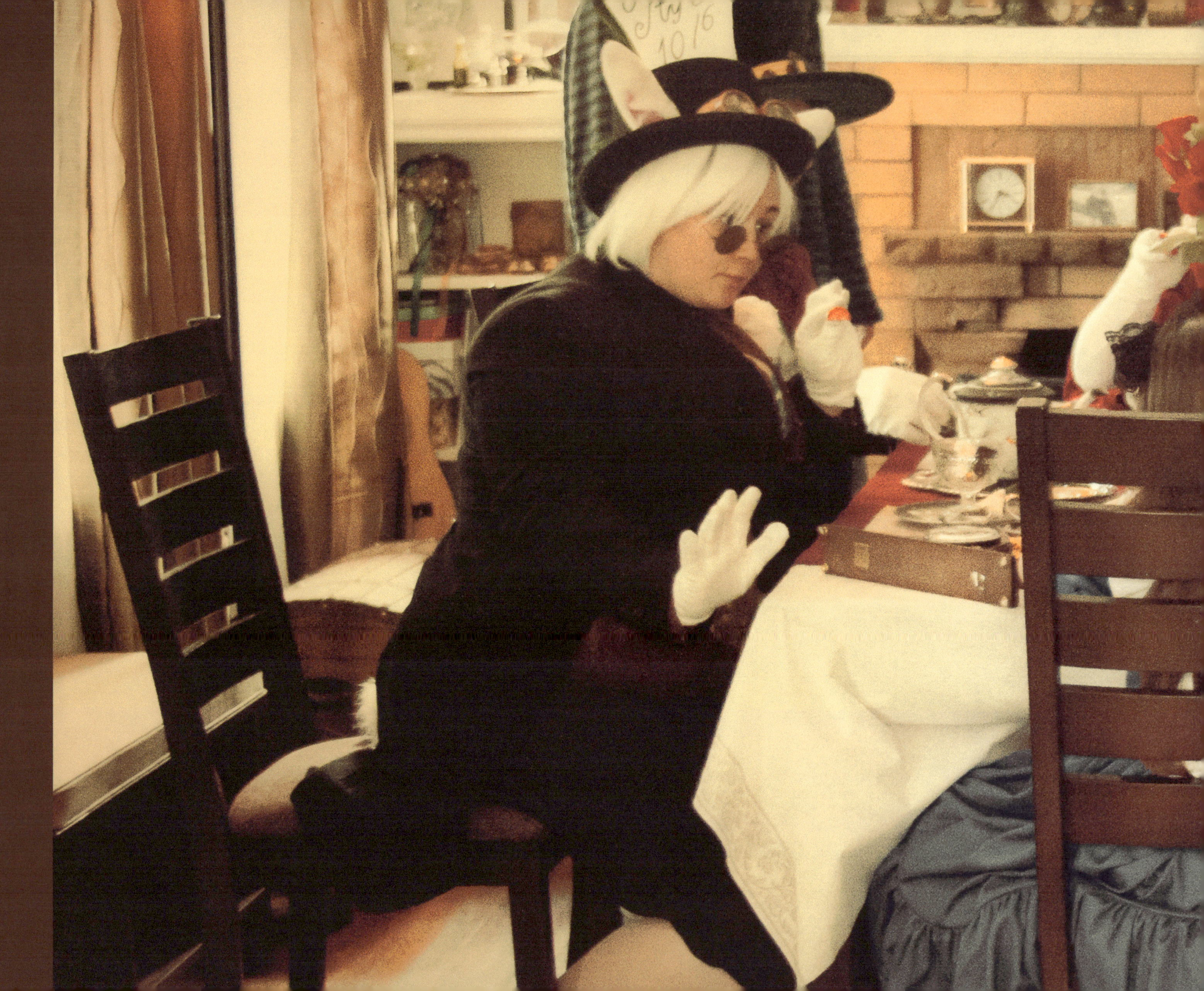

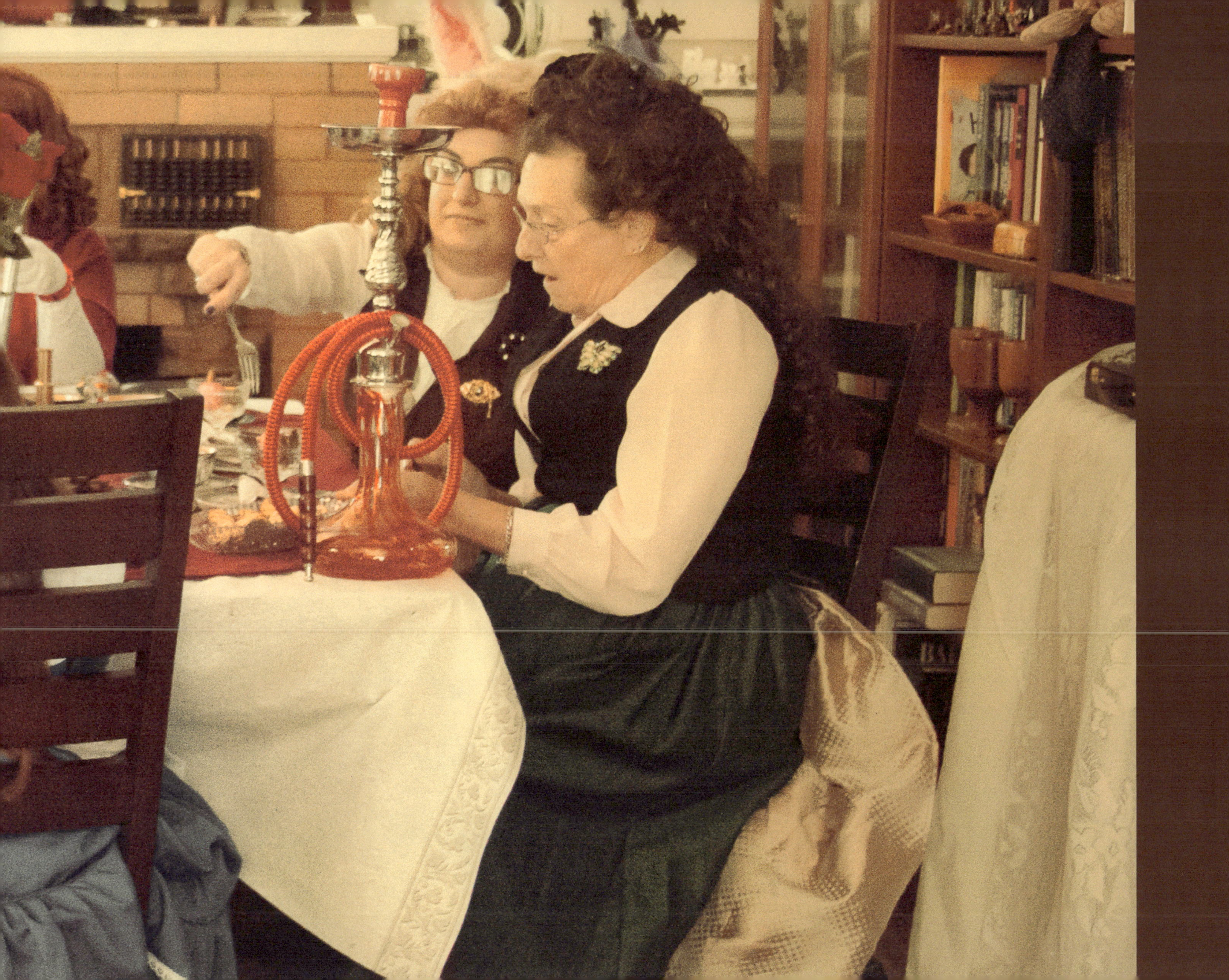

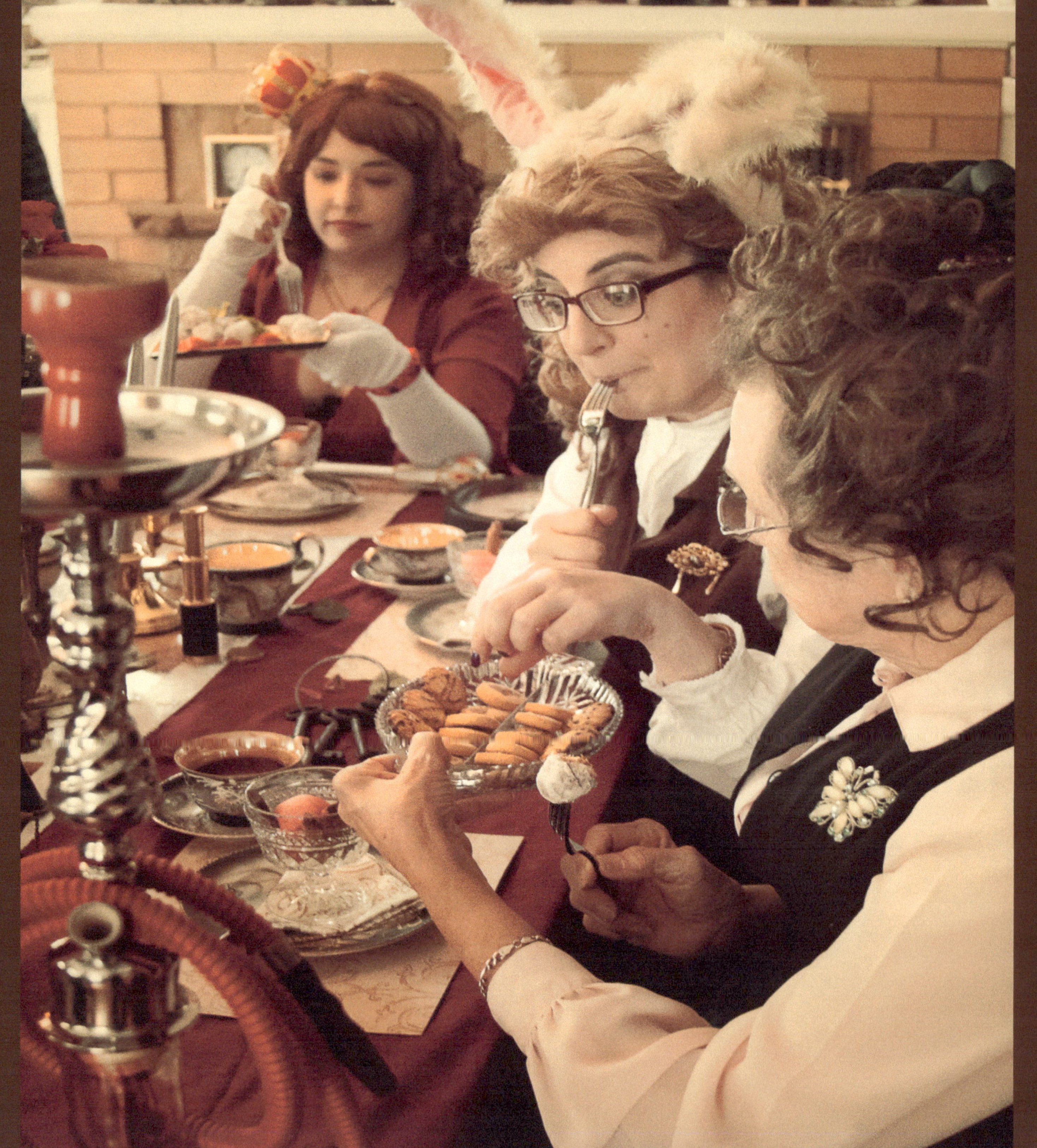

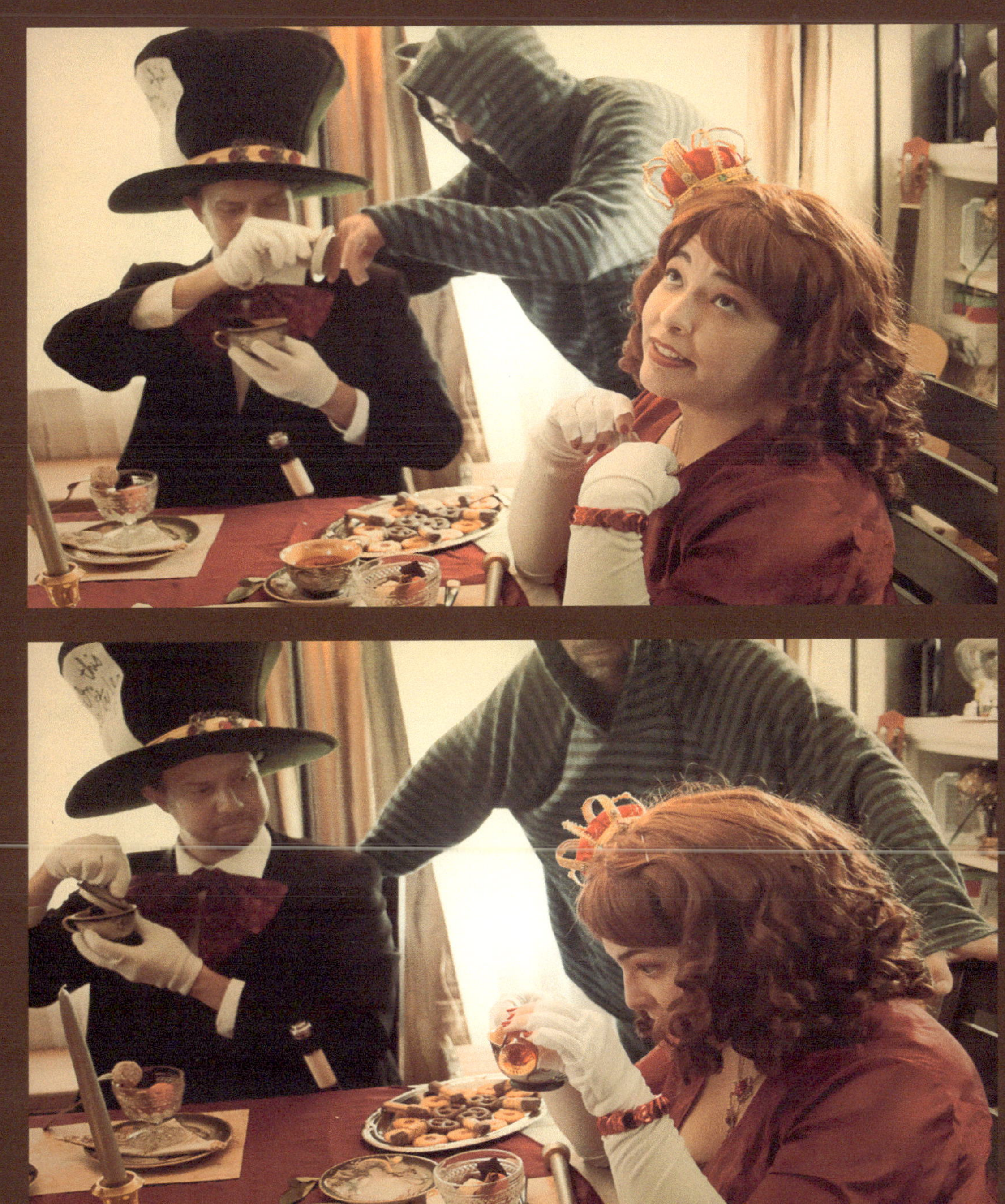

"Sometimes I wonder why I do this to myself . . ."

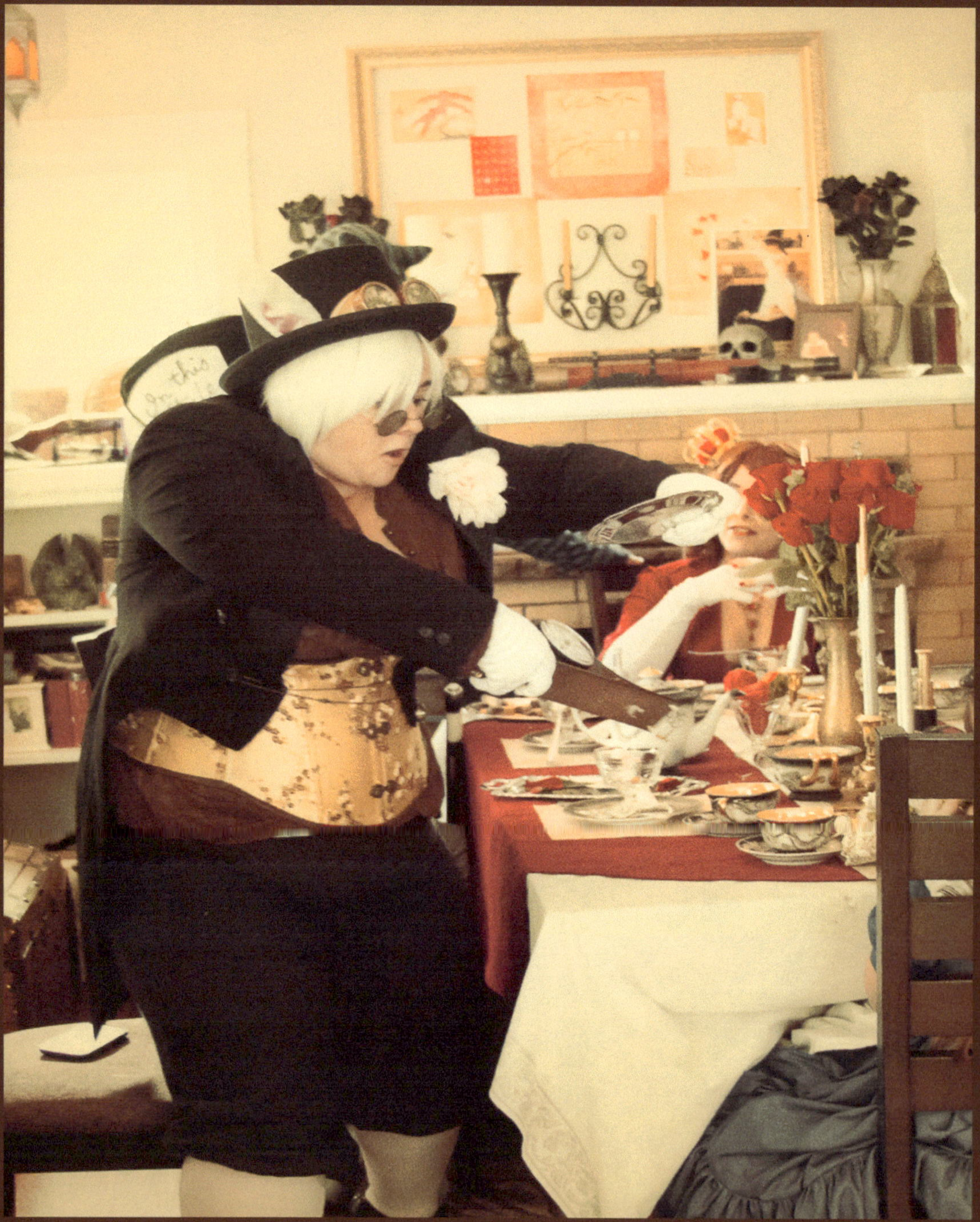

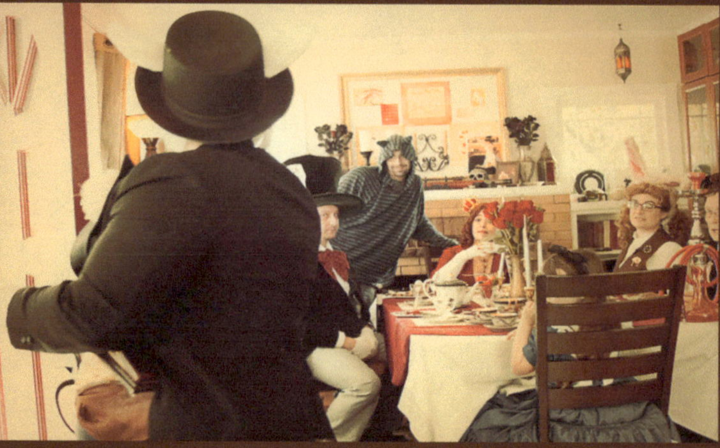

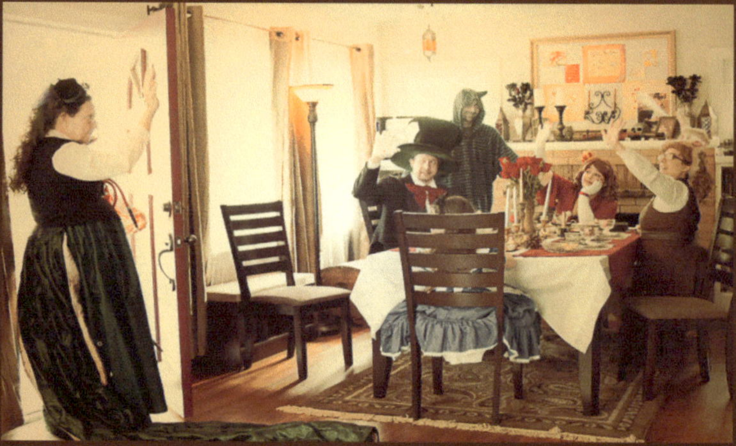

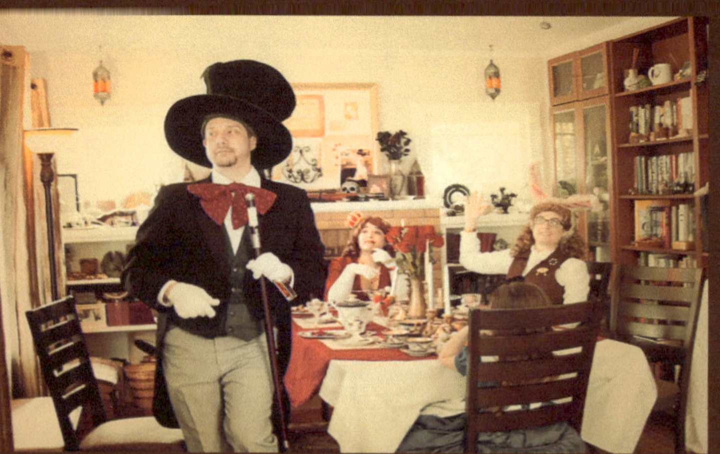

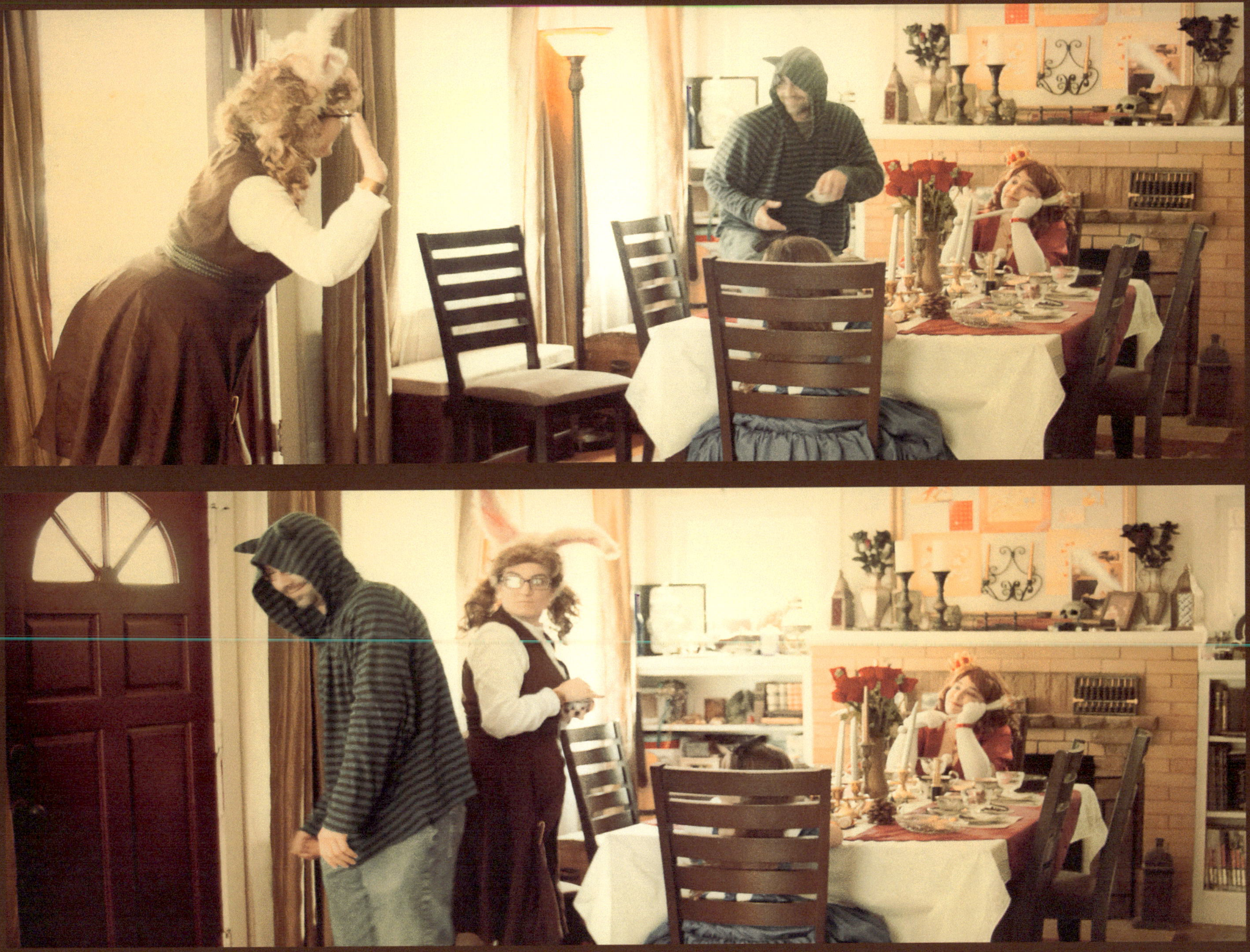

"The Dormouse stays! Out with you, Cheshire."

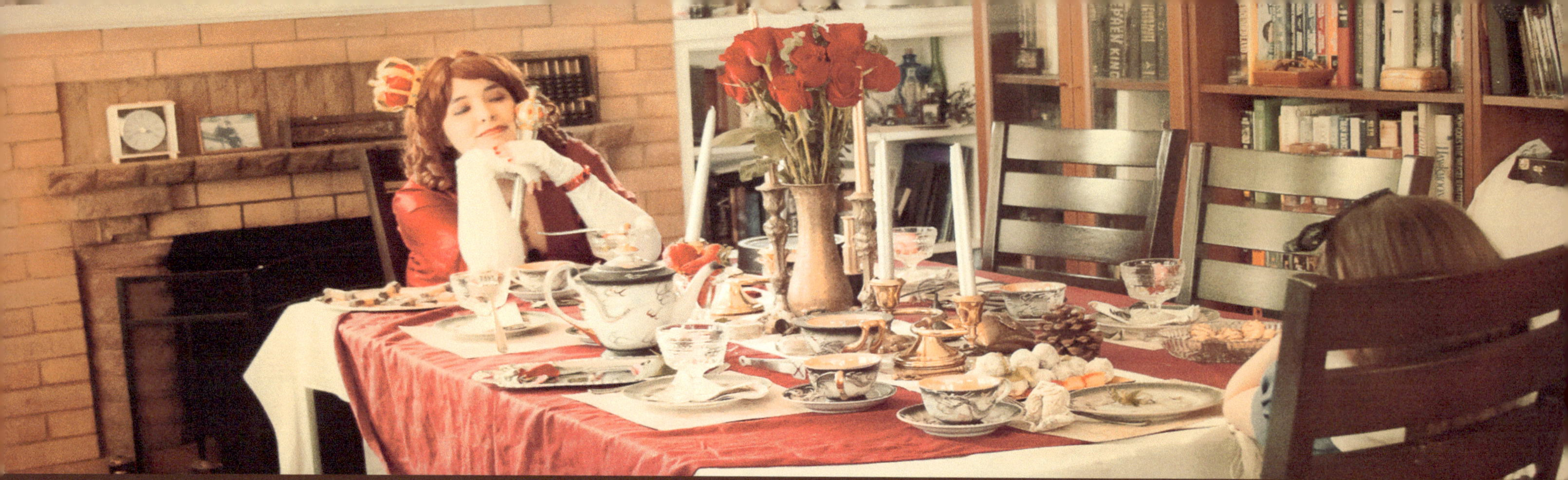

"Have you ever?"
"Ever what?"
"Exactly. Now do be a dear and clean up the table."
"How do I get myself into these things . . .?"

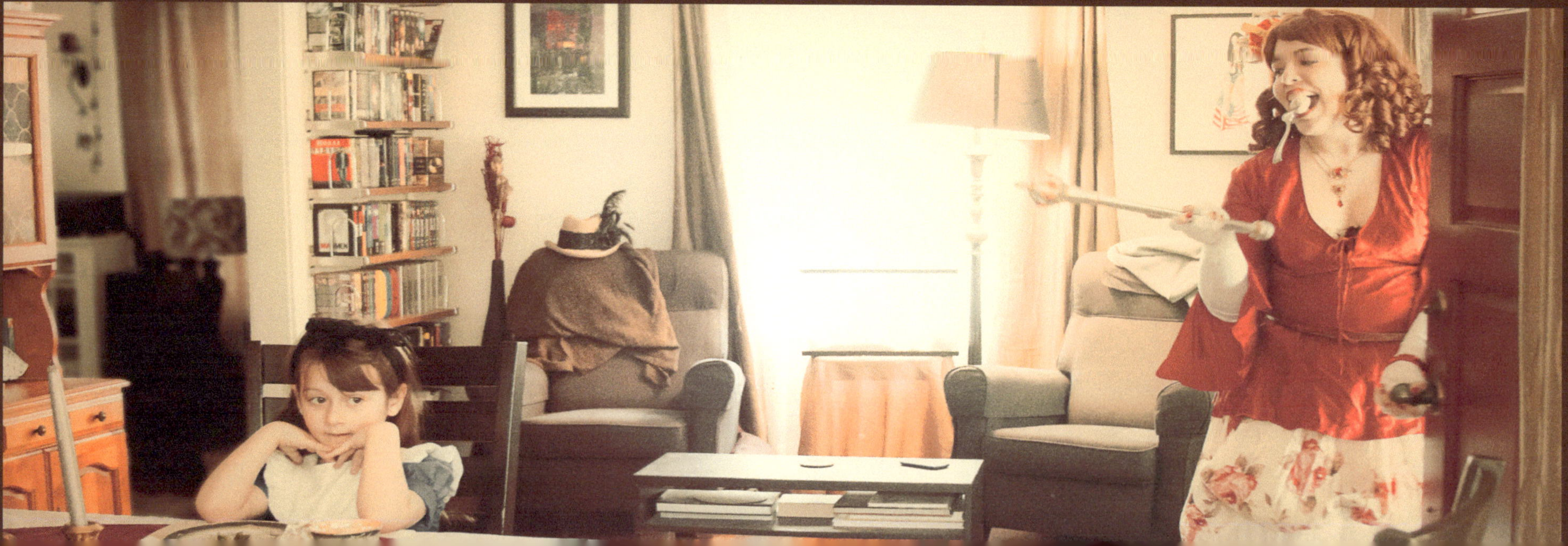

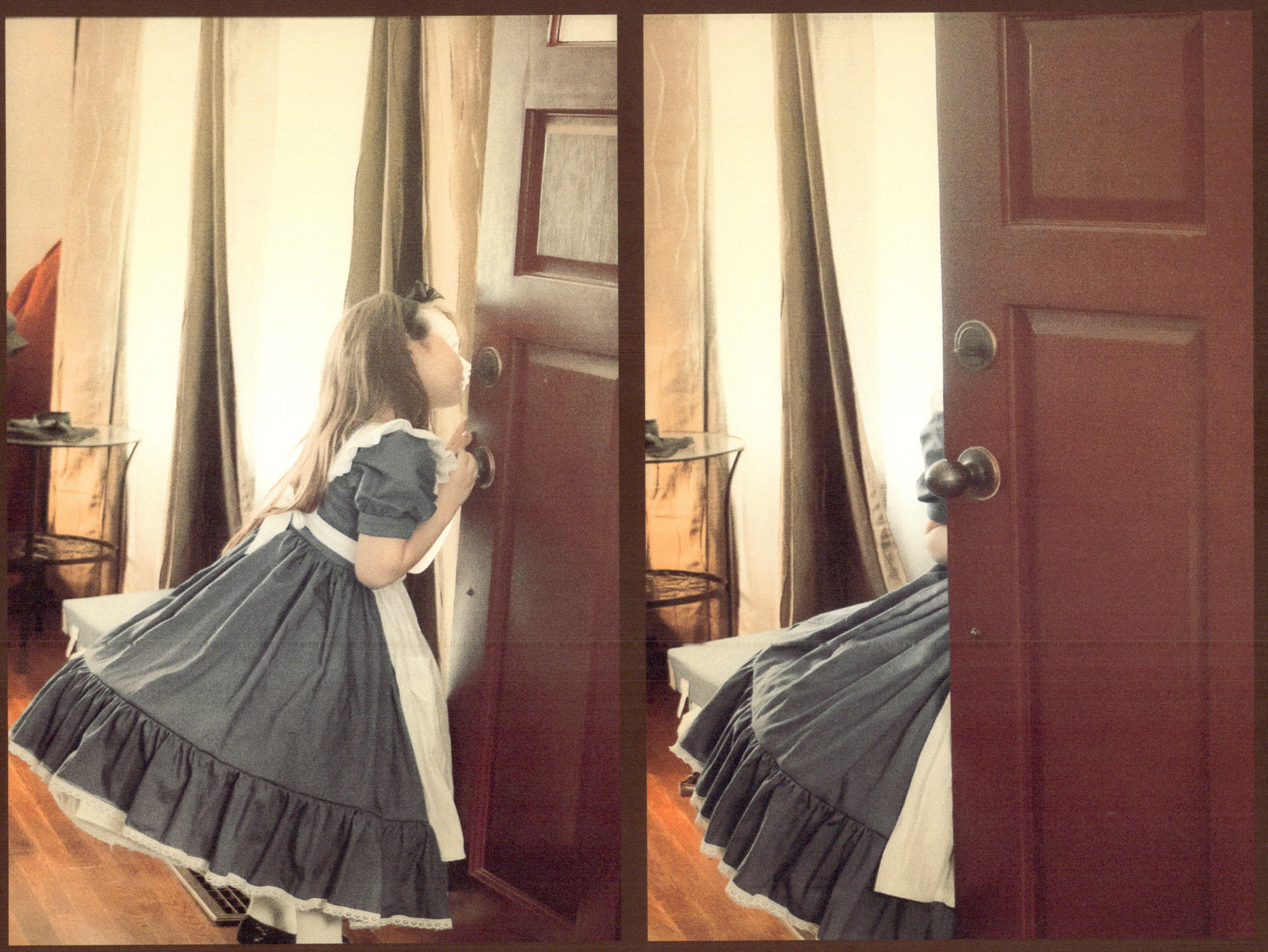

"Such a curious place I found. I wonder where I shall go next."

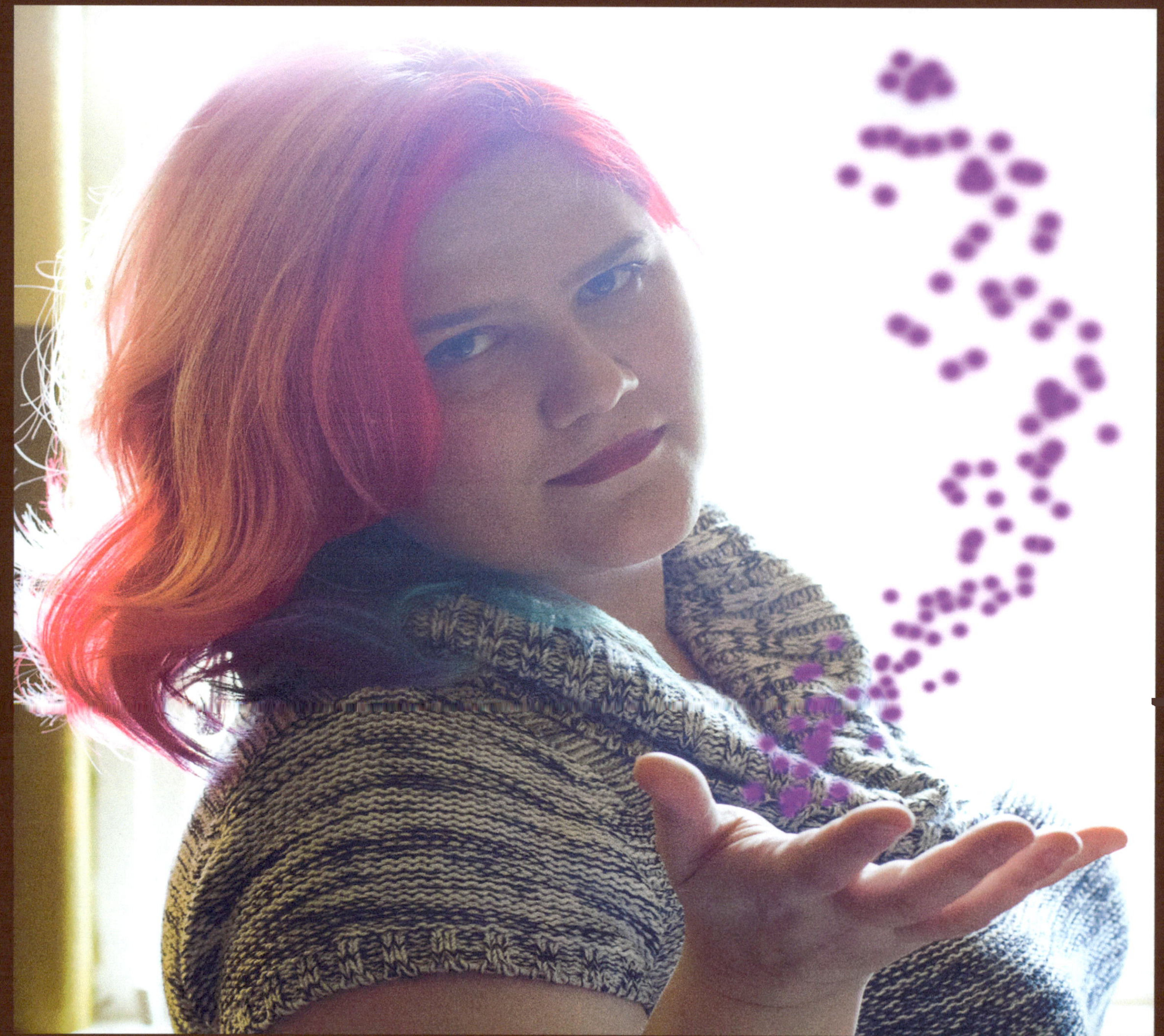

Stacy J. Garrett (S. J. Garrett) was made in England but born in Sacramento, California, and like the redwoods of the state, her roots have dug deep. Her destiny as a bard was somewhat inevitable. Little else can explain how she constantly told her mother tall tales so outlandish that she couldn't even get grounded for them. Her mother and grandmother had her reading by age three, and that love of a good story propelled her through so many books that Scholastic Books gave her a medal. At the age of twelve, she picked up a point-and-shoot camera, and her love of telling a story took itself on a new journey as she starting taking photographs no one believed an untrained child could. She entered junior college by age fifteen to study photography, and in the same year, she wrote her first story. She has never looked back.

Stacy has seen both good and evil in her life, and her works, like life, have no half measures. Even in fantasy worlds of dragons and faeries, she knows that the constants of real emotion never change. Whether shooting photographs in stark straight black and white or brilliant digital color, or turning out fantastical novels of over a hundred thousand words, she shows an ability to move hearts, engage minds, and take people beyond the borders of reality into another world entirely.

Her current haunt is a comfy house in her beloved Sacramento where she wrangles four feline fur-kids and consumes peppermints like mana in order to balance a calendar filled with more creative venues than a sane person should realistically undertake. She considers herself extremely blessed to be surrounded by a group of amazing friends and associates who never hesitate to volunteer to do something a little strange for the sake of art, whether it is getting almost naked in a park or dressing up for a steampunk tea party.

She holds an Associate of Arts Degree in Fine Arts Photography, as well as a Bachelor of Fine Arts in Photography. She will graduate in 2019 with her Masters of Fine Arts in Photography.